"What in t here?"

Jack folded his arms over his chest. "Sheer accident. I'm in town on business, and who do I see getting into a cab? The woman who walked out on me six months ago without so much as a goodbye. And now, for some reason, everyone thinks I'm your...husband?"

Rachel squeezed her eyes shut. "Please, Jack. Will you just go?"

"Oh, no. If you're going to pass me off as your husband, I've got a right to know why."

"It was a harmless little...ruse. That's all."

He eyed her carefully. "Why me?"

She turned away. "The picture was handy."

"Is that the only reason?"

"What other reason would there be?"

Jack gave her a cocky grin. "I'm unforgettable?"

Rachel shot him a look of disgust. Oh, he was *so* arrogant. And *so* conceited. And *so* right.

Dear Reader,

I've always loved those crazy stories where somebody tells a tiny fib, only to have that little falsehood escalate into a problem of major proportions!

In *Risky Business*, architect Rachel Westover is desperate to land her dream job, but the big boss refuses to consider unmarried job candidates. She decides that Jack Kellerman, a fun, sexy, captivating man with whom she once had a scorching one-night affair, can become her *imaginary* husband, since he lives a thousand miles away and will never know. She gets the job. Her plans works perfectly.

Then, out of the blue, Jack shows up at her office, quite amused that he appears to be married but can't seem to remember his wedding.

When everybody takes Jack to be her real husband, Rachel is forced to spend four days with him on an employee/spouse retreat at a romantic ski resort. Soon her one little fib has spiraled completely out of control. How can she, a serious, career-driven woman, be falling for a wildly spontaneous man who never takes *anything* seriously?

I hope you enjoy *Risky Business*. Visit me on the Web at www.janesullivan.com, or write to me at jane@janesullivan.com. I'd love to hear from you!

Best wishes,

Jane Sullivan

Books by Jane Sullivan

HARLEQUIN TEMPTATION
854—ONE HOT TEXAN

HARLEQUIN DUETS
48—THE MATCHMAKER'S MISTAKE
33—STRAY HEARTS

RISKY BUSINESS
Jane Sullivan

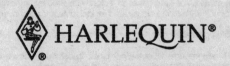

HARLEQUIN®

TORONTO • NEW YORK • LONDON
AMSTERDAM • PARIS • SYDNEY • HAMBURG
STOCKHOLM • ATHENS • TOKYO • MILAN • MADRID
PRAGUE • WARSAW • BUDAPEST • AUCKLAND

To my sister Mary Ann,
my most enthusiastic fan.
Thanks for loving my books, and for telling
everyone else on the planet that they will, too.

ISBN 0-373-69098-3

RISKY BUSINESS

Copyright © 2002 by Jane Graves.

All rights reserved. Except for use in any review, the reproduction or
utilization of this work in whole or in part in any form by any electronic,
mechanical or other means, now known or hereafter invented, including
xerography, photocopying and recording, or in any information storage
or retrieval system, is forbidden without the written permission of the
publisher, Harlequin Enterprises Limited, 225 Duncan Mill Road,
Don Mills, Ontario, Canada M3B 3K9.

All characters in this book have no existence outside the imagination of
the author and have no relation whatsoever to anyone bearing the same
name or names. They are not even distantly inspired by any individual
known or unknown to the author, and all incidents are pure invention.

This edition published by arrangement with Harlequin Books S.A.

® and TM are trademarks of the publisher. Trademarks indicated with
® are registered in the United States Patent and Trademark Office, the
Canadian Trade Marks Office and in other countries.

Visit us at www.eHarlequin.com

Printed in U.S.A.

1

JACK KELLERMAN WAS A BORN optimist.

He couldn't remember a time in his life when he hadn't believed that the glass was half-full. That when a door closed, a window opened. That things always worked out for the best, that tomorrow was another day, and that life really was a bowl of cherries. And above all, that laughter was indeed the best medicine.

But even at his most positive, no way could he have predicted a day like today.

He'd caught an early morning flight from San Antonio to Denver. Nonstop. Arrived ten minutes early. Actual breakfast on the plane rather than a package of stale dry-roasted peanuts. Sat down next to a woman with a baby, and the child fell asleep when they took off and didn't even wake when they landed. Gorgeous redhead from San Antonio in the seat to his left, literate, well-spoken and maybe even telling the truth when she said she was unmarried. She'd slipped her card into the pocket of his leather jacket as they got off the plane, giving him a smile that said, *Anywhere, anytime, any way*.

As he exited the terminal, he got a picture-postcard view of the snowcapped Rocky Mountains in the distance. He picked up a cab with a functioning heater. The driver, who actually spoke English, drove him into downtown Denver, where a light sprinkling of snow blanketed the sidewalks with a soft white powder.

And now, as Jack stood inside the lobby of the Fairfax Hotel, turning a slow circle and taking in every nuance of the late-nineteenth-century architecture and decor, he couldn't help smiling. He'd wondered whether this trip would be worth it. He wasn't wondering now.

Man, oh *man*, what a beautiful sight.

He checked his watch and saw that he was thirty minutes early for his appointment with the hotel manager. He stepped into the lounge, slid onto a stool at the bar and watched as a blonde sitting at the other end of the bar uncrossed her legs, then crossed them again, giving him an inviting smile.

Nice. *Very* nice.

The only thing that rivaled Jack's passion for historic places was his passion for beautiful women. And right now, he was experiencing the best of both worlds.

He returned her smile, knowing it never hurt to plant seeds. If she was still here by the time the manager finished giving him a tour of the place, he might just have himself a lunch partner. Maybe more. If this day got any better he wasn't going to be able to stand it.

But business first. Then pleasure.

The bartender came by, and Jack asked for a cup of coffee. Then he pulled out his cell phone, tapped number one on the speed dial, and after a few rings, Tom came on the line. His cousin and business partner, Tom was holding down the fort in San Antonio while he made the trip to Denver.

"You at the hotel already?" Tom asked.

"Just got here."

"Well? Is it everything we thought it would be?"

"More. It's a gold mine. Crystal chandeliers, oak and mahogany floors, brass fixtures all over the place, and enough stained glass to fill the Vatican."

"Wow. Sounds good."

"It's better than good. I can't believe some idiot wants to demolish it."

"Yeah, but their loss is our gain."

Jack had to admit that was true. Their business was historic renovation, not demolition, but if they couldn't stop the destruction of buildings like this one, at least they could salvage the interiors for use somewhere else. Still, the lack of foresight of some people really grated on Jack's nerves. A fifty-story office complex might be the highest and best use of this property if a person was looking at it from strictly a financial viewpoint, but once those explosives were planted and detonated, a piece of history would be lost forever. How could anyone put a price tag on that?

Jack glanced back at the blonde, who was toying with a cocktail straw and not even trying to hide the fact that her attention was focused squarely on him. He didn't have to be back at the airport until seven o'clock tonight. A lot could happen in seven hours.

"How long do you think it would take to pull everything out of there?" Tom asked.

"Hard to say. I'll know more after I go through it. Trouble is, they want the building on the ground before the end of February."

Tom let out a breath of frustration. "That could be cutting it close."

"We could bring two crews up here."

"That'll short us on the Wimberly Building."

"But that one has a longer fuse. We can afford that."

"This all assumes we win the bid."

"I'm telling you, Tom, if the rest of the place is as good as what I've seen so far, I'll make sure we win the bid."

The blonde picked up her glass of wine and took a sip,

then teased her lower lip against the rim in a provocative back-and-forth motion. He was getting exactly the right kind of vibes from her—vibes that told him she wanted nice conversation, great sex—and a no-strings-attached goodbye.

Maybe they'd skip lunch in the restaurant and go straight to room service.

"So when is your meeting with the manager?" Tom asked.

"Eleven-thirty. I'm a little early, so I thought I'd—"

Jack stopped short. Looking out the window to the street beside the hotel, he saw something that froze him to the spot where he sat.

No. It couldn't be.

He sat motionless, his heart suddenly beating rapid-fire, as he watched a woman on the sidewalk. She held shopping bags in both hands, her purse tossed over her shoulder, looking as if she wanted to hail a cab. Even at this distance, he could see the smooth, ivory skin of her face in contrast to the crimson of her lips, both framed by black-as-night hair that swirled in the winter breeze.

Hadn't he touched that face before? Kissed those lips? Run his fingers through that hair?

It was her. Rachel.

No. That was wishful thinking. The woman he'd known in San Antonio had been all long legs and luscious curves and warm, soft mouth, and every move she'd made had been a sensual feast for the eyes. This woman was wearing a conservative wool coat with a hem below her knees, black gloves and black low-heeled shoes, look-ing so sharp and conservative that if a Marine recruiter had happened by, he would have dragged her straight to boot camp. Would the woman he'd known in San Anto-nio have dressed like that?

He wasn't sure. He'd have to think hard to remember what she looked like with clothes on.

They'd spent one night together—one hot, exciting, unforgettable night—only to have her leave before daybreak without so much as telling him her last name. Not a day had passed in the last six months that he hadn't thought about her, and he'd held out hope that someday he would see her again. And now, as he looked at this woman, the most uncanny feeling of recognition took him by the throat and refused to let go, telling him that today just might be that day.

"Jack?" Tom said. "Are you there?"

Tom's voice had become as comprehensible as a mosquito buzzing in his ear. The blonde gave him yet another provocative smile, but that didn't register, either. Every molecule in his body was tuned toward the woman on the sidewalk outside, and all at once the promise he'd made to himself that morning six months ago came back to him like a prophecy just waiting to be fulfilled.

He'd told himself that if he ever saw her again, he'd never let her go.

"Sorry, Tom. Gotta run. I'll call you back later."

"Hey! Wait! You haven't finished telling me—"

Jack hit a button on the phone and stuffed it back into his coat pocket. He reached for his wallet, grabbed the first bill he saw—a ten—and tossed it onto the bar. The blonde gave him a surprised look, but he was already off his bar stool and heading out of the lounge.

He ran into the lobby, glanced out the window again and panicked when he didn't see her. He burst through the revolving door onto the sidewalk, the cold winter wind slapping him in the face, just in time to see her pulling a cab door closed behind her.

"Rachel!"

He ran toward the cab, shouting her name, but the

wind caught his words and blew them right back at him. The cab pulled away from the curb.

He spun around and ran to another cab, leaped inside, slammed the door and pointed madly. "Follow that cab!"

The driver, a gray-haired guy who seemed to be moving in slow motion, looked at him as if he was out of his mind.

"I know," Jack said impatiently. "Cliché. Just do it anyway, will you?"

The man shook his head and hit the gas, accelerating quickly to keep the cab ahead of them in sight. It was no small task, since its driver seemed hell-bent on setting a new land speed record.

"Stay with him," Jack said.

"Lots of traffic. I'll give it a shot."

By going five miles over the speed limit, the driver managed to stay just one car behind the other cab. And the whole time, Jack was consumed by thoughts of the day he'd met Rachel and the incredible hours they'd spent together.

That afternoon he'd gone by the Alamo in downtown San Antonio, partly because he had a little time to kill, and partly because it was one of his favorite places. She'd been out by the well behind the chapel, one of the only buildings in the Alamo complex left standing. He was first struck by her beauty, but it didn't take long for him to discover that much more lay beneath her surface. After only a few minutes of conversation, he realized she knew more about the Alamo than he did, and that was saying a lot.

After spending a good two hours talking about nineteenth-century history, Jack had been positively entranced. Later they'd had dinner together, then strolled along the Riverwalk. And then they'd done something that was impulsive even for him.

As evening turned to dusk, their walk took them past

the old Stonebriar Hotel. He didn't know who made the first move toward it, but looking back, their thoughts had been so in tune that he imagined they must have done it together. Within minutes they'd checked in. He'd barely waited until they'd gotten into the elevator before he kissed her, and it was all they could do to get down the hall to their room before they came together in a fiery sexual encounter that made every other experience he'd ever had with a woman pale by comparison.

Then he'd awakened the next morning to find her gone. No note, no phone message, no nothing. And he realized that while they'd talked endlessly about history, she'd sidestepped more personal conversation, leaving him with only three pieces of information about her: Her name was Rachel, she was from out of town and she was an architect. And that was it. And from that day forward, he'd fervently hoped that somehow, someway, someday, their paths would cross again. How could he have known it would be a thousand miles away in Denver, Colorado?

All at once, the cab they were following accelerated, weaving hard to the right, then to the left, putting two more cars between them.

"You're losing them!" Jack told the driver.

"The guy's a maniac," he muttered. "I'm doing the best I can."

Jack yanked two twenties out of his wallet and held them up. "You need to do better."

The driver had a sudden change of attitude and stomped the gas. "Hang on."

With a little creative maneuvering of his own, Jack's driver managed to gain on the cab ahead of them. Every muscle in Jack's body was tense, every nerve ending alive. He had to catch up to her. He had to.

Then the light at the next intersection turned yellow. Jack's driver slammed on the brake and brought their cab to a tire-squealing halt, while the other cab crossed the intersection and buzzed away.

"Damn!" Jack said, smacking the back of the seat with his fist. He couldn't believe this. He couldn't believe he'd come so close to finding her, only to lose her again. He slumped back against the seat, still cursing under his breath.

"Hey!" the driver said, "It's stopping half a block up!"

Jack sat up again, hope surging through him. Looking down the street, he saw that the cab had pulled up next to the curb and the woman was getting out. Her straight dark hair swung across her shoulders as she bustled herself and her packages through the door of a high-rise bank building.

The light changed. Jack's driver hit the gas, and a moment later he pulled up to the curb in front of the building into which she'd disappeared. Jack tossed him money, then leaped out of the cab and raced into the building. Scanning the lobby, he spotted her standing in a crowd near the elevators.

As he sprinted toward her, a set of elevator doors opened and she got on. The crowd followed her, leaving just as big a crowd behind waiting for the next elevator. He pushed his way through the people with as much civility as he could given his desperation, getting dirty looks left and right. But he had to catch that elevator.

The doors were closing.

"Rachel!" he shouted.

He reached over the shoulder of a man in front of him and tried to wedge his hand between the doors.

"Hey, buddy!" the guy said. "Back off! The elevator's full!"

The doors closed, and the elevator began its ascent. Another came, and the people turned and hurried toward it, leaving Jack standing there alone, cursing his luck. Or lack of luck. This was a forty-story building, and thousands of people worked here. How would he ever find her?

He pulled out his cell phone and dialed. In a moment he had the manager of the Fairfax Hotel on the line and told him something had come up and he'd have to re-schedule his tour for later in the day. The man sounded a little annoyed, but Jack couldn't have cared less.

Then, as he stuffed the phone back into his pocket, he remembered that he did have one piece of information about Rachel. If she'd been telling him the truth about her profession, she was an architect.

He strode back through the lobby, found the building management office, and a few minutes later he got what he was after: the names and addresses of five architectural firms housed within the building.

He returned to the elevators, his body humming with anticipation, images of Rachel swirling through his mind. She was beautiful, but the world was full of beautiful women, and his attraction to her had gone way beyond that. Even though their time together could have been counted in hours, for maybe the first time in his life he'd been thinking about the possibility of making a relation-ship permanent.

He'd find her. One way or the other, before this day was out, he'd find her. And if he had his way, he'd have her back in his arms again.

2

Rachel Westover got out of the elevator on the thirty-eighth floor, then turned and backed through the glass door of Davidson Design, dragging two large shopping bags along with her. If this day got any worse, she wouldn't be able to stand it.

She'd realized this morning as she was leaving for work that she really could use a couple of new sweaters and a few other things if she intended to go to a ski resort for the next four days. So she'd ventured out for an early lunch hour, fought the crowds at both Ann Taylor and Express, stood in line next to a woman with a screaming baby, paid far too much for everything because she had no time to shop for a bargain, then took a cab back to her office driven by a guy who didn't know the meaning of the word *brake*.

But at least now she was ready for the retreat. Four days of skiing in Silver Springs, courtesy of the big boss, Walter Davidson. The man liked to promote a "one big, happy family" feeling among his employees, and occasional employee/spouse retreats were his way of making that happen. Rachel had never been very comfortable in social situations, particularly those which she was forced to attend, so she wasn't looking forward to this one. Unfortunately, turning down such a generous invitation would make her look ungrateful. And with the new project manager position opening up, she definitely didn't want to appear that way.

The receptionist, Megan Rice, an animated little red-head with big brown eyes, peered over her desk.

"Hey, Rachel. Have fun shopping?"

"Not in the least."

"Aw, come on. It's always fun to spend money."

Not for Rachel. Saving money was fun. Spending it was painful.

The phone trilled. Megan punched a button on her console, answered it, then routed it with another touch of her fingertip. Most companies had done away with call-routing receptionists and gone to voice mail. But Walter Davidson insisted on maintaining the personal touch, and Megan manned the central nervous system of Davidson Design with astonishing proficiency. She greeted visitors, did overflow word processing and generally took up slack wherever she found it. But despite her obvious competence, there was something about her that had always made Rachel feel just a touch uneasy.

Maybe it was the barbed wire tattoo on her upper arm that occasionally peeked out from under her sleeve. Maybe it was the glint in her eyes that said she always knew *way* more than she was saying. Maybe it was the phone calls she made sometimes to somebody named "Blade." But for one reason or another, Rachel had come to suspect the truth: lurking behind those big brown eyes was the heart of a hell-raiser.

And now the hell-raiser was smiling at her.

Under normal circumstances, Megan's smile was just a smile. But today was Rachel's birthday. Megan was the self-appointed celebrant of all birthdays on the premises, and she accomplished that duty in ways that struck fear in Rachel's heart. Rachel hated people making a fuss over her. But when it came to birthdays, Megan went beyond fuss and edged right into human torture.

A bouquet of black balloons.

Candles that wouldn't blow out.

A six-foot rabbit belting out a singing telegram.

A T-shirt that read, I'm Not Old, I'm Chronologically Challenged.

"Any messages for me?" Rachel asked.

"No," Megan said with a smile. "But I have something for you."

Oh, no.

Rachel glanced quickly over one shoulder, then the other. She saw nothing suspicious, but that didn't mean a thing. It could come from anywhere at any time, so she had to stay on her toes.

"Please, Megan," she said. "I know it's my birthday, but—"

"Hey, calm down, will you? It's no big deal."

That hardly made Rachel feel better. Megan thought a dancing chimpanzee was no big deal.

"Please," she said imploringly. "Just tell me..." She took a deep, calming breath and let it out slowly. "Just tell me it's not a stripper."

Megan looked horrified. "You're kidding, right? *A stripper?* Would I *do* something like that?"

The answer was an unqualified *yes.* A stripper. A guy with a boom box and a G-string beneath his tearaway pants, ready to bump and grind his way through a routine that would make Madonna die of embarrassment. Everyone would come out of their offices to watch the show, and she'd have to tolerate it or look like a bad sport.

That Walter allowed such behavior amazed Rachel. But it was just one more expression of his core ideology: the employees who played together stayed together, and if a few practical jokes masquerading as birthday surprises enhanced that mood, he was all for it.

Rachel sighed inwardly. What had happened to work-places where people were stuffy and uptight and gave out birthday cards with rhyming verses that weren't dirty limericks?

Then Megan reached for something underneath her desk, and Rachel braced herself.

"Here you go," Megan said, and set a cupcake on the counter. Rachel held her breath, eyeing it warily. A cupcake? Surely there was more to it than that.

"Lighten up, will you?" Megan said. "It's *way* too small for a stripper to jump out of."

True.

Rachel let out the breath she'd been holding. Well. That wasn't so bad. A nice, conservative cupcake topped with white frosting and a single pink candle. That she could deal with.

"I know you said you didn't even want a cake," Megan said, "but everybody needs a cake on their birthday. Even if it's a little one."

"Well...thank you, Megan. I appreciate that."

Megan motioned to the end of the reception desk. "And those roses are for you, too. They came while you were out to lunch. Aren't they something?"

Ah. The flowers. They'd arrived. And they were some-thing, all right. Just the kind of flowers sent by a man crazy in love with his wife.

"Yes," she agreed. "Jack is very sweet. I've told him time and time again that flowers are a silly waste of money, but he won't listen."

"Too bad he couldn't make it back to town for your birthday."

"He tried to catch a flight out, but he couldn't. It's a

long way from South America, you know, and the access is pretty bad. He has to take a flight whenever he can get one."

Megan rested her chin on her hand. "Wow. It must really be tough to have your husband gone all the time."

Rachel let out a theatrical sigh. "I do miss him."

"Easy to see why," Megan said with a smile. "He's gorgeous. Well, his picture is, anyway. Are we ever going to get to meet him?"

"Sure. Someday soon. I promise."

Actually, the real answer to that question was *Not in a million years*. But Megan didn't know that. Neither did anyone else at Davidson Design. And they never would.

Megan flicked a lighter and lit the candle on the cupcake. "Go ahead. Make a wish."

That was easy. Rachel closed her eyes, then blew out the candle.

Megan leaned in close and whispered, "You wished for the promotion, didn't you?"

Of course she had, but she didn't particularly like Megan pointing it out.

Ever since her firm had won the bid to design a glitzy new hotel in Reno, she'd been evaluating her chances to become project manager. Her only real competition was Phil Wardman, a man with far less experience and technical ability than she had. But he had something she didn't. Phil happened to be one of those backslapping, buddy-buddy kind of guys that Walter Davidson just loved. They talked sports, sometimes even played golf together, and more than once Rachel had seen them going out to lunch. Personally all that familiarity made her uncomfortable. After all, what did any of that stuff have to do with a person's ability to do a job?

Over the next four days at the ski resort, she hoped to

tip the scales in her favor, finding subtle ways to suggest to Walter that she really was the best candidate. In the end, she had to trust that any sane person would promote someone with qualifications over someone with schmooz-ability.

"Actually," Rachel told Megan, "I wished for my husband to make it home in time to come on the retreat with me." She sighed again. "But I'm afraid that's not going to happen."

"Maybe next time." Megan punched a button to answer a call, staring pointedly at Rachel. "And then we'd actually get to meet him."

Rachel smiled indulgently, then, gathering up her shopping bags, the flowers and the cupcake, went into her office. She deposited the bags on the floor and placed the roses on her desk—one dozen American Beauty roses that had cost way more than she ever should have spent. But they were exactly what her sweet, loving husband would have sent her.

Her sweet, loving, *imaginary* husband.

Rachel sat down in her chair and traced her finger over the wedding ring on her left hand, which contained a stone just big enough to be impressive, but small enough not to be ostentatious. They could do wonders with cubic zirconia these days. Unless somebody pried it off her finger and held it under a jeweler's loupe, nobody would ever suspect that it wasn't a real diamond.

And then there was the photograph, the one she and Jack had asked a passerby to take of the two of them on the Riverwalk in San Antonio. She'd had the photo enlarged, framed it and placed it on her credenza. And because she'd created just the right profession for Jack that explained why he was rarely in town, nobody got suspicious as to why they'd never met him.

The ring, the photo, and a flower delivery every once in a while—that was all it had taken for everyone here to believe that she was actually married.

Okay, so it was a little deceptive. But the moment she'd heard of the job opening at Davidson Design six months ago, she'd wanted it desperately. A small firm with a hot reputation—what better place to make her mark? Then she'd gotten word through the grapevine that Walter Davidson had a strong preference for married job candidates, a qualification that was a little difficult to acquire on short notice.

So she'd faked it.

In the end, she'd gotten a job she loved, and Walter Davidson had gotten a talented, dedicated architect, who was going to help him put his small but growing firm on the map. Nobody was hurt. Her plan had worked perfectly.

She sighed. Okay. There was one tiny little glitch. She'd underestimated the way she would feel every time she looked at that photograph.

She turned slowly and stared at it, playing back in her mind the one night she and Jack had spent together. She remembered every moment of it—every kiss, every touch, every whispered word in the dark. He'd made her feel as if she were somebody else entirely—a hot, wanton, reckless woman who never met a sexual position she didn't like, a woman who would throw modesty and respectability and good behavior to the four winds and engage in a hedonistic sexfest that would have made a Roman emperor blush.

And it had scared the hell out of her.

She remembered with painful clarity how she'd felt when she woke before dawn and realized what she'd done. Fortunately she'd had the good sense to walk out of that hotel and leave temptation behind. Just thinking about that night made her cheeks flush with embarrassment. What kind of woman has wild, breathless sex with a man she doesn't even know? Repeatedly?

A woman who can't resist a handsome face and a gorgeous body. A woman who lives in a fantasy world instead of reality. A woman who's not in complete control of her life.

She'd tried to tell herself that she'd felt some kind of connection with Jack after the day they'd spent together, a meeting of minds and not just bodies. Finally, though, she came to her senses and realized she was just deluding herself. Such self-deception was nothing more than an excuse to justify her outlandish behavior.

What she couldn't figure out, then, was why she'd spent a good portion of every day since wondering what it might be like to see him again.

She had to stop this. She had her career to think about. The last thing she needed was to get waylaid by thoughts of a man who had undoubtedly put another notch in his bedpost before she'd even left the hotel. And seeing him again was a moot point, anyway. It wasn't going to happen. He was a thousand miles away in San Antonio. He could be her imaginary husband as long as she needed him to be, and nobody would be any the wiser.

And she would never have to be tempted by him again.

BY TWELVE-THIRTY, JACK HAD checked out four of the five architectural firms and come up empty. He'd found a few women named Rachel, but none that he recalled seeing naked in San Antonio.

The elevator doors opened on the thirty-eighth floor, and Jack stepped out. This was his last chance. If she didn't work for Davidson Design, he didn't know where to look next. He took a deep breath, opened the brass-trimmed glass doors and strode to the front desk. The receptionist, a bright, bubbly redhead with short, shaggy hair, held up her finger without glancing at him, asking him to wait as she answered one call after another.

Jack gazed around the room. Typical corporate look, with beige walls, modern art, leather furniture, track lighting. He decided he'd rather die and go to hell than be surrounded by this frigid atmosphere. At least hell would be warm.

And right in the middle of the ice box sat a leather-clad guy, his shirt open almost to his navel, with a neckful of silver chains and a couple of random piercings and tattoos. A boom box sat on the chair next to him. He leaned over and checked out his reflection in the coffee-table glass, patting a stray strand of blond hair back into place. He flipped his wrist and glanced at his watch, then *tap, tap, tapped* his fingertips against the arm of his chair.

"Hey, lady!" he called out to the receptionist. "I got a schedule to keep!"

The receptionist covered her mouthpiece and responded in a heavy stage whisper. "I told you it'll be just a minute! Will you keep your shirt on? At least until I tell you to take it off?"

With a disgusted shake of her head that made her short red hair flutter, she tapped a button on her console, then finally turned her gaze up to Jack.

"May I help—"

Her mouth dropped open. She froze in that position, staring at him, her eyes as big and bright as a pair of flashlight beams.

"*Dr. Kellerman?*"

Doctor?

"I can't believe it! You made it back!"

Made it back?

"Oh! Oh! You must be here to surprise Rachel!"

"Did you say Rachel?" His heart leaped with hope. "Late twenties, straight dark hair, blue eyes—"

"Well, of course!"

The woman yanked off her headset, tossed it aside and leaped to her feet, scurrying around the desk. "She's not going to believe this. She's simply not going to believe it. *Oooh!* What a wonderful surprise!"

She spun around and pointed to the kid in the waiting area. "You! Never mind! I don't need you after all!"

The guy leaped to his feet, his silver chains jangling. "Hey! I've been waiting here for fifteen minutes, and now you're telling me—"

"I'll send you a check!"

Before leather boy could protest further, the receptionist grabbed Jack by the arm and dragged him down a short hall, then stopped suddenly and pushed him up against the wall, her eyes wide with excitement.

"Okay. You stand here. Just wait here until I give you the word, okay?"

"I don't get this. What are you—"

She put her fingers to her lips and shushed him, then held up her palm. "Just wait here. This is going to be *so* cool!"

This place was a loony bin. Or, at least, this woman was loony. And he was pretty sure the guy in the waiting room had a screw loose, too. What in the world had he walked into?

The receptionist pushed the door open and strolled into the office, downshifting her voice into a soft, professional tone.

"Excuse me, Rachel. Do you have a moment?"

"I'm really busy, Megan. Can it wait?"

"No, I'm sorry," Megan said, her voice edged with excitement. "It can't wait. Your *real* birthday present is here."

Jack heard a gasp.

"Oh, no."

"Oh, yeah. And you're gonna love it."

"No, Megan. I'm warning you. The cupcake was plenty. Don't you dare do something weird. Do you hear me? Don't you dare—"

Megan's hand snaked around the doorway, found Jack's arm, and yanked him into the office. The moment his eyes met Rachel's, she leaped up out of her chair so suddenly that it rolled backward and smacked against her credenza.

Looking at her up close now, he knew. It was Rachel. No question about it.

Not that he would have recognized her by the clothes she wore. After the weekend they'd spent together, he would have expected to see her in something significantly more daring than the drab wool suit and buttoned-up white silk blouse she had on right now. Something brighter. Slinkier. Cut down to here and up to there. Something bold and carefree. Something that said, *Come here, if you dare,* instead of *Don't touch me if you value your life.*

But there was a part of her she couldn't hide behind those yards and yards of wool. Her eyes. He'd never forget those eyes as long as he lived, gorgeous ice-blue eyes that had kept him enthralled for hours on end.

But now they seemed to hold another quality. Surprise. No, not just surprise. Something more like...

Panic.

Megan patted Jack's arm. "I'd have put a big red bow on him, but I was fresh out of ribbon. Happy birthday, Rachel."

3

RACHEL'S BRAIN WAS TELLING her mouth that it really
ought to close itself, but the message simply wasn't getting through.

Jack Kellerman. Her imaginary husband, in the flesh.

Oh. My. God.

"Hello, Rachel."

That voice. Rich. Resonant. A voice just made for seduction. Only one of many reasons that she'd been so easily...seduced.

"Your husband!" Megan gushed. "Can you believe it?
All of a sudden I looked up, and there he was! He traveled
four thousand miles to surprise you on your birthday!
Isn't that just the most romantic thing ever?" She gave
Jack an appreciative once-over, then stage-whispered to
Rachel. "His picture doesn't do him justice."

"Picture?" Jack said.

"The one on her credenza. She stares at it all the time.
Now I know why."

Jack's gaze flicked over to the photograph. Rachel felt
her cheeks flush hotly, an anatomical glitch she'd been
cursed with since childhood. Like a pair of internal humiliation indicators, her cheeks became ripe tomatoes
whenever she was embarrassed. And Jack noticed it. How
could he not? She didn't remember one single part of her
body that had escaped his scrutiny six months ago, and
nothing was escaping him now.

Absolutely nothing.

Jack eyed the photo for a moment, then looked back at Rachel. When his brows dipped down with a confused expression and he opened his mouth to speak, she knew he was only a few words away from turning her career into toast.

"Jack!" she said. "I can't believe you're here!"

She circled her desk, rushed toward him, threw her arms around his neck and whispered in his ear. "Play along. *Please.*"

Then she tried to ease away from him, but to her surprise, he pulled her right back up against him, holding her as if he hadn't seen her in weeks and was making up for lost time.

"I've missed you," he murmured. "Have you missed me?"

She stared at him, wide-eyed. "Uh...of course. You know I have."

A smile eased across his face. "Aren't you going to kiss me?"

Kiss him?

Rachel swallowed hard, knowing she had no choice. She gave him a quick peck on the lips, and his face fell into a disappointed frown.

"Oh, sweetheart," he said. "It's been so long. Surely you can do better than that."

She inched toward him again, but this time, as her lips approached his, he tucked her head into the crook of his elbow, bent her backward, and showed her exactly what kind of kiss he was talking about.

Rachel's heart leaped wildly as his mouth fell against hers. Her lips had parted in a tiny gasp, and that small opening was all he needed to ease his tongue into her mouth, twining it sensually with hers. At the same time, he slid his free hand beneath her suit coat and around her waist, splaying his fingers against the small of her back. He held her firmly, possessively, demandingly—kissing her in a way that could bring a dead woman back to life.

And Megan was watching the whole thing.

If Rachel had any inclination to pull away, that stopped her cold. After all, Megan thought Jack was her loving husband, back from a long trip. Wouldn't she *want* him to kiss her?

Yes. Of course. She had no other choice. She had to let him kiss her.

And kiss her.

And kiss her.

Aeons seemed to pass before he finally pulled her to her feet and eased his lips away from hers. He gave her a suggestive smile, and out of the corner of her eye, she saw Megan's expression of absolute astonishment.

"Wow," Megan said, her mouth hanging open. "I mean...*wow*."

Rachel eased out of Jack's grip, feeling as if he'd literally taken her breath away. She gave her suit coat a nervous tug, then smoothed it with her hands, trying to look as nonchalant as possible. Tall order with Jack still looking at her as if he was only one moment away from clearing the top of her desk with a sweep of his arm, then hurling her down on top of it and having his way with her.

"Megan," Rachel said, "I'd like to be alone with Jack for a few minutes. If you'll excuse us?"

"Well, of course," Megan said. Then she leaned in and said quietly, "Hey, if you want to lock your door for a little while, I'll just tell everyone you're in a meeting."

"Not *that* kind of alone!"

"I don't know," Jack said. "Sounds like a pretty good idea to me."

Every word he uttered in that gorgeous, hot-as-sin voice made all kinds of provocative images fill Rachel's mind. She remembered lying in the darkness of that historic San Antonio hotel room, listening to Jack whisper a litany of sex talk that had set her on fire. What he wanted to do to her. What he wanted her to do to him. What they were going to do to each other. *All night long.* And right now, if she hadn't been terrified of the massive lie she was getting ready to be caught in, she'd have melted right into the carpet.

"We want to *talk*," she told Megan.

"Gotcha," Megan said. "Have fun...talking."

She gave them a little wave of her fingertips and a great big smile, then eased out the door. Rachel spun around to face Jack.

"What in the *hell* are you doing here?"

He folded his arms over his chest, those green eyes sparkling like crazy. "Well, from what I can tell, it appears I'm here to wish you a happy birthday."

"You have to leave. Now!"

"Are you kidding? I just traveled four thousand miles to be with you on your birthday."

She closed her eyes, willing herself to remain calm. "How did you find me?"

"Sheer accident. I'm here in Denver on business, and who do I see getting into a cab? The woman who walked out on me six months ago without so much as a goodbye."

No. This couldn't be happening. *No.*

"And now, for some reason," Jack went on, "your receptionist seems to think I'm somebody else. She's got the Kellerman right." He raised his eyebrows. "But there's this little matter of my being your...husband?"

Rachel squeezed her eyes closed. "Please, Jack. Will you just go?"

"No. I don't think so. Not just yet."

He looked at the photograph on her credenza again, then strode over to the flower arrangement on her desk. Before she could stop him, he picked up the card. Rachel buried her face in her hands.

"To my darling Rachel," he read aloud. "Sorry I can't be with you on your special day. I'm counting the minutes until we can be together again. Your loving husband, Jack." He turned back to her with a smile of pure delight. "Damn, I'm romantic. Didn't know I had it in me."

"Just put it back, will you?"

He returned the card to its place, then turned and leaned against her desk. "Okay. Suppose you tell me what's going on here."

"Just leave. That's all I want you to do."

"Oh, no. If you're going to pass me off as your husband, I've got a right to know why."

She waved her hand dismissively. "It was just a harmless little...ruse. That's all."

"Ruse?" he said. "Lie, you mean."

"No! Well, yes. I mean—" She exhaled sharply. "It was for my job, okay?"

"Go on."

She put her hand to her forehead for a moment, then met his eyes again. "When I applied for it, I found out the big boss, Walter Davidson, prefers his employees to be married. Stability, and all that. So I...well, I guess I gave him what he wanted."

"A married job candidate."

Rachel sighed. "Yes."

"And you obviously got the job."

"Yes."

"So now you're a married woman."

"As far as what everyone around here thinks, yes."

He nodded down at her hand. "Nice ring."

She slipped her hand behind her back. "It's cubic zirconia."

He winced. "Couldn't you have sprung for the real thing? I don't want people thinking I'm cheap."

"They're not thinking anything about you! You don't exist!"

He looked down at himself. "I look pretty real to me."

"You know what I mean!"

"And what's with the 'doctor' thing, anyway?"

Rachel buried her face in her hands again. Oh, God. Did she have to tell him this?

"It's why you're gone all the time," she said. "See, you...you fly to South America..."

"Yes?"

She thought she'd been so smart when she came up with this, but now she could barely say the words. She spoke quickly, mumbling so maybe he could hear only half the words. The ones that didn't sound stupid.

"You're an independently wealthy doctor who flies to poor South American countries on humanitarian missions."

His eyebrows flew up, and then a grin spread across his face. "You're kidding, right?"

She shot him a look of total disgust.

"Wow. I'm spontaneous, romantic, rich and charitable. No wonder you married me."

"Will you *stop* it?"

He eyed her carefully. "Why me?"

She turned away. "The picture was handy."

"Is that the only reason?"

"What other reason would there be?"

He gave her a cocky grin. "I'm unforgettable?"

Rachel shot him a look of disgust. Oh, he was *so* arrogant. And so conceited.

And *so* right.

Why had it been Jack's picture? So she could look at him every day of her life? So she could remember what that night of fantasy had been like before she'd had to wake up to reality?

"I'm sorry I did this," she said. "Believe me, I am. But you can't tell anyone." She looked at him warily. "You're not going to tell anyone, are you?"

"If anybody asks, I'm Dr. Jack Kellerman, wealthy philanthropist. Your husband." He eased closer, tucking a strand of hair behind her ear. "Assuming, of course, that the job comes with conjugal rights."

Rachel gasped. "You think just because I told a little fib, it entitles you to—"

"No entitlement," he said. "I'm thinking of it more as...a perk."

Just as she was on the verge of going totally ballistic, the door to her office swung open. She spun around, expecting to tell Megan one more time to please leave them alone. Instead Walter Davidson walked into her office.

Rachel felt as if her stomach had dropped right out of her body and plummeted thirty-eight floors. *No, no, no!*

Walter, a balding man in his late fifties with a big, booming voice, zeroed in on Jack and strode across the room toward him with his hand extended.

"Rachel! Megan told me you had a visitor! So this is your husband?"

This was it. Her life was over.

But to her surprise, Jack didn't even look flustered. He met the man halfway with a broad grin and shook his hand.

"Dr. Kellerman," Walter said, pumping Jack's hand up and down. "It's so good to finally meet you."

"Call me Jack."

"Jack it is. And you call me Walter. Rachel here seems to have been a little reluctant to share you with us. I'm glad you finally dropped by. Are you planning on staying in the country for a while?"

"Yes," Jack said. "For quite a while, actually."

"Good. That means you can join us on the retreat."

Rachel bit back a gasp.

"Retreat?" Jack said.

"Rachel didn't tell you? I'm taking all the employees on a ski trip to The Summit in Silver Springs tomorrow morning. Four days. Rest and relaxation. Of course, spouses are invited."

"Why, Rachel," Jack said, "you didn't tell me anything about a retreat."

Rachel just about choked. "I—I didn't think you'd be back in town. You...surprised me, you know."

"Yes. I suppose I did."

"I'd love to have you join us," Walter said.

"He can't!" Rachel said.

Walter recoiled with surprise.

"It's just that...well, it's just that I know how tired he usually is after his trips out of the country," she said, stammering like an idiot. "I know he'd probably just like to stay at home. Rest. You know."

"Rachel's right," Jack said. "She knows me so well. Whenever I come home from one of my trips, all I want to do is zone out. Relax. Take it easy."

Rachel breathed a sigh of relief.

"Which means that a trip to a ski resort would be exactly what I need. I'd love to go."

Rachel thought her heart was going to stop. This

couldn't be happening. It couldn't be. It was as if she was paying right now for every lie she'd ever told in her life. God had saved up and hit her with her punishment all at once, and boy, was it a doozy.

"Excellent!" Walter exclaimed. "I'm interested in hearing all about your work. That is, between ski runs. You do ski, don't you?"

"Of course."

"Glad to have you joining us. I know there are a lot of people who will be interested in meeting Rachel's husband. You've been somewhat of a mystery man around this office."

"And I'd love to meet them."

"Well, I suppose if you'd like, I can introduce you right now."

"No!" Rachel said.

Walter looked at her again with surprise.

"Uh...Jack is late for an appointment already." She gave him a pointed stare, warning him not to disagree. "He can meet everyone tomorrow."

"That'll be fine," Walter said. "We'll see you both tomorrow afternoon at the resort, then?"

"Yes," Jack said. "Thank you for the invitation."

Walter left her office, and she spun around to face Jack.

"Are you *completely* out of your mind?"

"Out of my mind? To accept a free four-day vacation in the company of a beautiful woman? Yeah, I'm nuts, all right."

"You are *not* going to be in my company!"

"Beg to differ. We're married."

"We are *not* married!"

"That lovely fake wedding ring you're wearing says otherwise."

"Just how do you intend to pass yourself off as my husband for four days?"

"You've been passing me off for six months. I figure four days will be no big deal."

"That's right! I've been doing it! I made you up, so I know what to say about you! You don't! You don't know you like I do!" Rachel put her hand to her forehead. "My God, that sounded insane."

Jack laughed. "Calm down, will you? It'll be fun."

"Fun? *Fun?*" She paced in front of her desk, waving her arms. "This is my career we're talking about! If anybody finds out—"

"Nobody's going to find out."

"I don't believe this. You think you can just walk in here, and—"

"What I think, Rachel, is that you've been using me for six months. I should at least be entitled to four days."

"I've been using your picture! Not you!"

"My identity."

"Not exactly. You're not a doctor."

"So you embellished. Was that my fault?"

"You can't come with me, Jack. You can't—"

"Really? Walter says I can."

"He thinks you're my husband!"

"Isn't that what you want him to think?"

"Yes! As long as it's your picture he's thinking it about, not you!"

He grinned. "You're right. You do sound a little insane."

This was a nightmare. An honest-to-goodness nightmare come to life.

"I'm going to tell them you had a medical emergency," she said. "I'll tell them you had to fly out suddenly—"

"Sorry, Rachel. You're not getting rid of me that easily."

He walked over and stood in front of her, his smile dimming. "Why did you leave?"

"What?"

"In San Antonio. I woke up and found you gone."

She turned away. "I don't want to talk about that."

He pulled her back around and took her by the shoulders, staring down at her with a gaze so hot it made her breath catch in her throat.

"One night wasn't nearly enough. I don't know why you left, but now that I've found you again, I don't intend to let you go."

"There's nothing between us, Jack. That night meant nothing."

"That night was absolutely explosive and you know it. Tell me you've had better sex somewhere else. Go ahead. Tell me."

She swallowed hard. "I—I've had b-better sex somewhere...else."

Well, those were the most unconvincing six words she'd ever spoken, and the tiny smile that came to his lips told her he knew it. Damn it.

"There are more important things in life than sex," she said.

"It sure seemed to be at the top of your list that night in San Antonio."

"I—I was drunk."

"After one margarita?"

"I can't hold alcohol."

"You seemed plenty sober to me. I mean, if you'd been drunk, could you possibly have climbed up on that bathroom counter and—"

"Stop! Don't say it!"

She shuddered out of his grip. God, she was going to die of embarrassment. Right here, right now.

His voice softened. "Why are you denying this? And why did you disappear?"

"Because that wasn't me! The woman I was that night—she doesn't really exist!"

"No, Rachel. Dr. Jack Kellerman, medical humanitarian, doesn't exist. But the woman I knew in San Antonio—the woman I touched, the woman I kissed, the woman with more erogenous zones than I could count—she was very real."

Rachel felt her cheeks flush red yet again. "Listen to me, Jack. Just because I took a side road one night doesn't mean that's the path I always travel. Or that it's one I ever intend to go down again."

"I see." He nodded thoughtfully. "So you're telling me that you don't want any more of the best sex you ever had. For four days. At a ski resort. With a fireplace, a beautiful view... Yeah, I see your point. That would be a fate worse than death."

"Stop it! Will you just stop it? I don't want you coming with me!"

"Sorry, Rachel. You've made your bed, and now you're going to lie in it." He grinned. "But don't worry. I'll keep you company."

Rachel remembered how spontaneous he'd been. How he'd teased and laughed and behaved in ways she'd found totally irresistible. It had all been very tantalizing when it happened between the sheets, but if he turned on those same characteristics full force around her co-workers and her boss, he could send her career up in flames. But there wasn't anything she could do about it. Nothing. He knew her secret, so he held all the cards.

"What time do you get off work?" Jack asked her.

"I need to stay until six o'clock tonight."

"Good. I'll be back then."

"You'll be back? Why?"

"So we can go home together. Where is it we live again?"

She held up her palm. "No. No way. You're not staying with me tonight."

"This was a day trip to Denver for me," he told her. "I haven't got hotel reservations."

"So make some."

"But we're supposed to be married. What would people think if they knew I was sleeping in a hotel?"

"No one will ever know."

"Has it occurred to you that once we get to that resort, we'll be sharing a room?" He raised an eyebrow. "Maybe even a bed?"

Rachel blinked with sudden realization. She hadn't thought of that. And now that she did...

She'd had her choice of a king-size bed in her room, or two double beds. Of course, she'd reserved the king—she certainly didn't need two beds. And how could she change it now? What woman wouldn't opt for a king-size bed over two doubles when she was sharing a room with her husband?

"Seems to me that in light of that upcoming arrangement," Jack went on, "my staying at your place isn't a big deal. Then we can go to the resort together tomorrow." He checked his watch. "Actually, I do have an appointment this afternoon, but I'll be back here by six o'clock." He opened her office door, then gave her a knowing smile. "Happy birthday, Rachel."

He left her office and closed the door behind him. Rachel stared after him in total disbelief, then sank into her chair, put her elbows on her desk and dropped her head to her hands. Oh, Lord, what was she going to do now? For the next four days, she was stuck trying to control a powder keg by the name of Jack Kellerman, a powder keg that could explode at any moment.

She took a deep, calming breath. Okay. She had to focus here. Goal number one: Keep Jack's identity a secret. Goal number two: Keep Jack's body out of her bed. Goal number three: Keep Jack's naked body out of her mind.

If she could pull off all three of those things, she just might escape from this outrageous situation with her career and her self-respect intact. If not...

Oh, boy.

She closed her eyes and promised God that if He'd just get her out of this one little pickle, she'd never tell a lie again.

4

AFTER LEAVING RACHEL'S office, Jack headed back to the Fairfax Hotel, where he met with the manager and got a tour of the place. Everything was as he'd expected it to be, and more. He called Tom, gave him some specifics, and told him to start working up a bid. Then he dropped the news that he wouldn't be back to the work site for a couple of days. Tom had gone a little nuts over that, but this trip wasn't negotiable. Business would keep.

Rachel wouldn't.

He certainly hadn't planned for things to go the way they had today, and he could hardly believe his luck. A four-day retreat? Sharing a room? And Rachel had to pretend he was her husband?

Did it get any better than that?

Okay. She clearly didn't want him around. Or she thought she didn't, anyway. But now he had four days to convince her otherwise. To put her into the same kind of atmosphere they'd experienced in San Antonio and see what might happen between them. If he could bring back just a glimmer of the connection he'd felt with her, it would all be worth it.

At the Fairfax, he begged for the use of a computer from the hotel manager's secretary. He researched the Web sites of humanitarian groups who flew to other countries to offer medical assistance, committing buzz words to memory that he could use if necessary. Rachel would undoubtedly fill him in on information concerning what she'd told the people she worked with. Then he'd mesh the two together and come up with a profile he could use so he wouldn't get tripped up. Even without the preparation, though, he wouldn't have anticipated any problems in that regard.

After spending his entire childhood as the son of a petroleum engineer who was transferred every year or two, Jack had lived all over the United States and in several foreign countries. He'd been forced to give up friends, then turn right around and make new ones so many times that he'd become a master of the game.

At first it had been painful. Then he discovered the secret. If he made the other kids laugh, pretty soon he had them eating out of his hand. Life could be pretty dull, and the person who spiced things up was the person who had a list of friends as long as his arm. He sometimes felt that he could parachute into anyplace on the planet, and within two days he could have a party and invite twenty people who'd be happy to come. Consequently, he'd never met a situation in his life that he couldn't talk himself into or out of, and this one would be no different.

After he finished his research, he went by a couple of downtown stores and picked up a few things. Ski equipment he could rent at the resort, but he needed enough clothes and other items to last him four days. He hadn't planned on going on a buying spree, but as an independently wealthy doctor, shouldn't he really look his best?

Then, at the appointed hour, he returned to Rachel's office. Her attitude toward him hadn't changed a bit. In fact, she acted so coldly toward him as they drove to her condominium that he wouldn't have been surprised to see icicles forming on the *inside* of her car. Once they got there, she parked her car, strode inside and didn't even bother to look back to see if he was following her or not. Jack just smiled. She couldn't hold out forever. Sooner or later, the sweet, congenial, sexually insatiable woman he'd known in San Antonio would rise to the surface, and when she did, he'd be waiting.

Then he went inside her condo, and he wondered if maybe locating her wild side again would be a taller task than he'd imagined.

Her decor consisted of off-white carpet and off-white walls. Generic art that matched the drapes that matched the sofa that matched the chairs. Not a speck of dust anywhere or a statuette out of place. Dreary traditional furniture that looked as if nobody had ever sat on it. Her home looked like a place where a person twice her age might live—a person twice her age with a desire to freeze the pants off anyone who stepped foot inside it. It reminded him of the decor he'd seen at her office today—modern, efficient, practical, heartless. If he'd found just one cracked wall, a mismatched pillow, or even a family picture or two, he might have been able to feel comfortable.

No chance of that.

Did the same woman live here whom he'd shared the room with in the historic San Antonio hotel? The one with the leaky clawfoot tub and the four-poster bed? The one with the cracks in the walls? The one she said she loved the very smell of?

Impossible.

Rachel hung her coat in the front closet, then did the same with his.

"Have you eaten?" she asked him.

"No, but I'd be happy to take you out."

She gave him a *yeah, I'll just bet you would* look, then strode toward the kitchen. "I'll order something."

"Order?"

"I don't cook. Not very often, anyway."

"Then what do you eat?"

"Yogurt and granola for breakfast. A salad for lunch. Anything ready to microwave for dinner. Low fat, low cal."

"How about a pizza?" he asked.

She winced. "I guess one without meat would be okay."

"I was thinking pepperoni."

Her lip curled, clearly showing her distaste. "Do you ever think of your arteries?"

"As little as possible."

"I don't blame you. They're probably a real mess."

"If you'll remember, we ordered room service in San Antonio."

She looked away. "So?"

"Steak and potatoes. Chocolate cheesecake for dessert. Extra whipped cream. In fact, as I remember, we talked the room service waiter into bringing us an entire *can* of whipped cream." He grinned. "Amazing what you can do with one of those, isn't it?"

Her cheeks flamed red all over again. She started to say something, then clamped her mouth shut, probably figuring that denial was pointless since she was the one who'd emptied most of the can.

She pulled open a kitchen drawer and grabbed a coupon. "Go ahead. Order pepperoni. Extra cheese. Stuffed crust. And why don't you get a bunch of those bread sticks while you're at it? The ones that you dip in garlic butter? That ought to really send the old cholesterol through the roof."

He smiled. "Now you're talking."

She rolled her eyes with disgust. Slapping the coupon

on the counter, she went into her bedroom and closed the door behind her. Jack sighed and shook his head. He knew at heart she was a pepperoni pizza eater, but now was not the time to push the issue. He grabbed the phone, dialed the number of the pizza place and ordered a vegetarian supreme.

By the time the pizza got there and they ate, it was approaching eight o'clock. No matter how often he tried to start a conversation, Rachel rebuffed him at every turn. If she couldn't stop him from coming to the resort with her, she clearly intended to make their time together as unpleasant as she possibly could. That was okay. He wasn't blessed with an excess of virtues, but patience was one he had in spades.

After they finished eating, Rachel sent him to the living room, then cleaned up the kitchen. She then disappeared down the hall, brought back sheets, blankets and a pillow and lay them on the sofa. She returned to her bedroom. A moment later, he heard a shower running.

Well. So much for an evening of pleasant conversation. Or great sex.

Okay, the "great sex" thing had been a real long shot. But a guy could always hope.

Figuring he'd seen the last of her tonight, Jack located a TV behind the doors of an armoire. He pulled out the remote, ran the dial, stopped on a few things that he thought might be interesting only to find he really didn't give a damn.

Finally he flipped the TV off, then got up and inspected her bookshelves, where he found all the latest titles of the day—Oprah picks, up-to-the-minute nonfiction, a few classics, a pristine coffee-table volume of modern architecture. On a wall next to the bookshelf hung two diplomas, indicating that she had both a bachelor's degree and master's degree in architecture from an institution he recognized as a prestigious women's college.

Women's college. He'd often wondered what kind of people went to a place for four years where they spent all day without ever setting eyes on a member of the opposite sex. He'd had a nightmare like that once. It wasn't pretty.

Then he glanced down the hall and noticed a second bedroom. Guest room? Probably not, since he was sleeping on the sofa. Then again, she *was* out to punish him.

He walked quietly down the hall. The door was ajar. He pushed it open and peered inside.

A desk sat along one wall, a drawing board in the corner. More bookshelves. But the books they contained were hardly literary masterpieces or full of contemporary buzz. Most of them were history texts and books on architecture of all periods—ancient, medieval, eighteenth and nineteenth century—mostly used books with ragged covers. And the balance of the titles were fiction, mainly mysteries and romance.

Yes. This was more like it. He had the distinct impression that the books in the living room with the unbroken spines were the ones she showed to the world, while these tattered ones lived in her heart. Then he turned and got another surprise.

That day in San Antonio, they'd browsed through the Alamo gift shop, where he'd bought her a poster of an 1830s map of Texas. Here it was, matted, framed and hanging on the wall.

He remembered so clearly the time they'd spent there, perusing every document, every artifact. To find a woman with that kind of knowledge of the historical periods that fascinated him had pleased him to no end. That he was attracted to her in every other way possible made him feel as if he'd found the perfect woman. A soul mate, and he didn't even believe in such things.

And then she'd disappeared.

"What are you doing in here?"

He spun around. Rachel was standing behind him, wearing a blue terry-cloth robe that gave a new meaning to the word *frumpy*. He knew a really hot body lurked under there somewhere, but he sure as hell couldn't see it right now.

He shrugged. "Just looking around."

"Well, don't."

There it was again. That crimson flush on her ivory cheeks, as if somehow he'd embarrassed her.

"The poster," he said. "It looks good."

She turned instantly and left the room. He followed. She started to go into her bedroom, but he caught her arm and pulled her back around.

"Hey, hold on. What's the matter?"

She looked up at him, her pale blue eyes brimming with annoyance. "It's bad enough for me to look up and find you standing in my office this afternoon. Then you beg your way into my house. And now you're snooping around."

"I wasn't snooping."

"Then what do you call it?"

"The door was open."

"That room is private!"

She looked genuinely angry. "Okay. I'm sorry. I shouldn't have gone in there."

"That's right. You shouldn't have."

"But I can't imagine why you wouldn't want me to. The rest of this place isn't you. That room is."

She ducked her head, the color still hot on her cheeks. "You don't know anything about me."

He inched closer to her and placed his palm on the wall beside her head, dropping his voice. "Yes, I do. Maybe a whole lot more than most people do. That day in San Antonio, and then that night, I found out all kinds of things about you."

"You have to stop this."

"What?"

She closed her eyes. "Reminding me."

"You don't want to be reminded?"

"I did a very dumb thing that night, something I'd just as soon forget."

"So that's the way you remember it? As something you want to forget?"

"Yes."

"You even want to forget how we met? The time we spent together that afternoon?"

He saw the indecision on her face. Was she going to acknowledge the truth, or continue to act as if their entire encounter had been the biggest mistake of her life?

"No," she said finally. "That was nice."

"Ah. Finally something we agree on."

"But I wasn't looking for a relationship then, and I'm still not looking."

"I didn't know we were talking about lifetime commitments here."

"I don't even want a four-day commitment from you. I don't want anything from you. In fact, if you'd just go back to San Antonio and leave me alone, I'd be the happiest woman alive."

"No, Rachel. I know what would make you the happiest woman alive, and it has nothing to do with me going back to San Antonio." Slowly he dropped his head and placed a gentle kiss against her neck, then brought his lips up to brush against her ear. She was tense—so tense—and he wanted nothing more than to kiss all that tension away, for her to melt in his arms again.

"Let her out," he whispered. "Right now. Show me that woman I knew in San Antonio."

"Jack—"

"She's in there," he said. "I know she is. A beautiful, sexy woman I can't wait to touch. We can be together again the way we were before, just the two of us, for hours on end—"

"No!"

She twisted to the left, then ducked beneath his arm and strode back down the hall.

Damn.

He thought about stopping her, then thought again. More than anything, he wanted to follow her into her bedroom, slip that frumpy robe off her shoulders, kick it aside, then make love to her until daybreak. But even if he managed to accomplish that tonight, he had the feeling she'd only wake up tomorrow morning as wary as she'd been in San Antonio, and he definitely didn't want that. If he pushed her too hard right now, he could end up odd man out for the next four days, and there was no way he was going to let that happen.

As she reached her bedroom door, he called out to her. "Don't you want to know what I was doing in Denver?"

She stopped, then slowly turned, eyeing him suspiciously.

"There's a hotel not too far from where you work," he said. "The Fairfax. They're tearing it down."

Her eyebrows flew up. "They're *what?*"

"Tearing it down. Every brick, every chandelier, every doorknob, every strip of oak flooring—"

"But I love that hotel! I have lunch there at least once a week. Why don't they just renovate it?"

"Because a new high-rise is going up in its place."

She stepped back toward him. "But how can they tear down such a wonderful old building?"

"With a few well-placed explosives."

"But all that history will be gone!"

"Not all of it. I'm bidding for the right to salvage the interior of the hotel."

Rachel's eyes lit up. "Oh! That's right! You do restoration! Can you use all those fixtures somewhere else?"

"Absolutely. I've got one project I'm working on now in San Antonio of the same vintage, and another one is coming up. I'll do something with all of the salvaged items eventually, or piece them out to other renovators who can put them to good use."

"I guess it's not the same as leaving the hotel standing, but at least you'll be saving parts of it, right?"

There it was. That smile. That animated expression. That look of sheer radiance when she talked about anything connected to history. For the first time since he'd walked into her office this afternoon, he saw a glimmer of the woman he'd met that warm, sunny afternoon in San Antonio.

"That's better," he said.

"What?"

"You're smiling. I was beginning to think you'd forgotten how."

She looked flustered and turned away.

"Don't stop now," he said.

"Jack—"

"History. You love it. We talked nonstop about it that day, remember? And the hotel we stayed in. That was a piece of history all by itself, wasn't it?"

"I—I have to go to bed."

He nodded. "Okay. I'll see you in the morning."

She looked at him suspiciously.

"Don't worry, Rachel. As much as I'd like to join you, I'm not going to force my way into your bedroom."

She seemed totally unconvinced of that. "You're not?"

"No. Tonight I'll just settle for the smile."

She looked flustered all over again. She turned and disappeared into her bedroom, clicking the door shut behind her.

He found it amazing that a woman of her obvious professional capability could be so rattled by a tiny compliment. There was so much contradiction in her that he could probably take a year out of his life and still not figure it all out. Still, he had a feeling that it would be a year well spent.

She could try to fool him. She could wrap herself in that god-awful robe, or in wool from head to toe, put every hair in place and surround herself with hideous decor, but still he knew the truth. A passionate woman lurked beneath that cool surface, and he had exactly four days to get her to come out. And once she did, he'd never let her hide herself away again.

5

RACHEL SPENT MOST of the three-hour drive to Silver Springs, Colorado, with her stomach in turmoil. She'd barely slept last night. Just the thought of Jack being anywhere near her, even if he was in the other room, made visions of hot sex flash through her mind. And that was the last thing she needed to be thinking about.

Right now he was lounging comfortably in the passenger seat, as if they really were married and they really were going on a vacation, with a maddening attitude of total and complete nonchalance. But his attitude was the least of what was making her so uneasy right now. It was the physical aspect of the situation—sitting side by side with him in a closed-in space for hours—that was what was making her crazy.

Jack stood at least six foot two, with a body that said he was no stranger to physical activity. She remembered that his construction company was a small one, which meant he probably pitched right in beside his employees. An image formed in her mind of him working in the San Antonio heat, his body glistening with sweat, his T-shirt adhering to every muscle of his shoulders and chest, his biceps bulging...

Stop it.

Not once in her life had she allowed herself to succumb to the cliché of swooning over a sweaty man wielding power tools, yet here she was doing it. That kind of attraction was for people like her sister, who hopped into bed with any man with a hot body and a smooth come-on. Actually her sister *married* any man with a hot body and a smooth come-on. After Laura's third divorce, Rachel thought maybe her sister ought to consider that possibly she was looking for the wrong characteristics in a prospective husband, but would she listen? Not a chance.

Still, being in such close quarters with Jack right now, Rachel couldn't get that hunky-guy image out of her mind. Maybe that was because she knew that his work wasn't the only thing he sweated over. She remembered a time when she'd sweated right along beside him. And beneath him. And above him. And—

She took a deep, calming breath. She had to get a grip here. It was time to focus. To plan. To make sure she did everything in her power to keep this man under control. Thinking about what he looked like naked only complicated an already complicated issue.

She'd coached Jack on the part he was getting ready to play, but true to his nature, all he did was make light of the whole thing, treating it as if it were a meaningless little game that her whole future wasn't riding on. All it would take would be one slipup, and the whole world would know she'd lied about being married. And if that happened, she'd have no choice but to crawl into a hole somewhere and die of humiliation.

"Let's go over it again," she told him. "We were married two years ago in Austin—"

"We've been over it three times already. Once was plenty. Fortunately you don't tell your co-workers much, so there wasn't much for me to learn."

"Just remember not to get freaked out if somebody refers to you as 'doctor.'"

"Actually, Rachel, I don't remember the last time I got freaked out about anything."

She believed that. Wholeheartedly. Nothing bothered this man. It certainly didn't bother him to join her on this trip when she'd made it absolutely clear that she didn't want him to come. He just smiled and said he was coming anyway, which was enough to make her wish for a handful of antacid.

As they drove, a light, fluffy snow began to fall. She turned on her windshield wipers, slowing her speed on the winding road. Then, moments later, they rounded a curve, and The Summit came into view.

Since her company had designed it, she'd been up here several times already, but as usual it took her a moment to orient herself to its sudden presence on the mountain landscape. The Summit was a four-hundred-room hotel that connected to a shopping mall, several restaurants and nightclubs, all within walking distance of the ski slopes. It sprawled along a steep hillside, then spilled out into the edge of the valley

"Well," Rachel said, "there it is. Impressive, isn't it?"

Jack sat up straight, the strangest look coming over his face. "Uh...yeah. I'm having some strong impressions, all right."

"What do you mean?"

"I thought the mountains were supposed to be bigger than the resort. You know. *Way* bigger."

"Before you say too much negative about this place, I think you ought to know that my company designed it."

"You're kidding."

"No. And I had a hand in it."

"Just one hand? Maybe I could forgive that."

"I worked mainly on the shopping mall. The atrium area in particular."

"Ah. A shopping mall. How nice." He said the words with unmistakable disgust.

"I take it you don't like shopping malls."

"Not when they screw up my view of the mountains."

"Okay. It's big. But the demographics were here for a major expansion. The client wanted to corner the market in Silver Springs."

"I think they cornered the market for the entire state of Colorado."

"Come on, Jack. Don't be shy. Tell me what you really think."

"I think it would look great on the Sunset Strip. Does it light up with neon at night?"

She pulled into a parking space near the lobby entrance of the hotel and brought her car to a halt. "No. It doesn't light up with neon at night. Actually it's quite beautiful."

"I'll have to take your word for that."

"Our client's studies showed that people like all the conveniences of home, including shopping malls. But you'll notice," she said, pointing toward the building, "there are log accents around the lobby entrance, and major landscaping was done to reincorporate the native flora."

Jack unhooked his seat belt and faced her. "You sound like you're giving a presentation to a client. If you want to sell me on the place, show me a ski slope, a stone fireplace, a comfortable sofa, any drink with hot rum in it, and lose all the bells and whistles."

"My, you're easy to please."

"Oh, yeah. And I'll need somebody to keep me warm."

"That's what the fireplace is for."

"Nope. That wouldn't keep me nearly as warm as I intend to be."

"Then I suppose you'll have to put on an extra sweater."

"What I've got in mind involves taking clothes off, not putting them on."

Rachel closed her eyes. Is this what it was going to be like for the next four days? Knowing Jack, there was no doubt about it.

But at the moment there was a more immediate danger to deal with: the possibility of running into her boss and co-workers with her imaginary husband at her side before she could get settled. But looking around the parking lot, then through the monstrous wall of glass into the lobby, she was relieved to see no one she knew.

"Let's go check in," she told Jack, opening her car door. "But be careful. I don't see anyone from my office right now, but they could be anywhere. At anytime. We have to stay on our toes."

"Will you take it easy? I can handle this. Let's see...what was it again? We've been married ten years, three kids, house in the suburbs—"

"Jack!"

He slumped with resignation. "Rachel?"

"What?"

"We're going to get along a lot better over the next four days if you quit taking every word I say seriously. Just lighten up, will you? Have fun?"

Fun. At this point, nothing on earth was further from her mind.

"If anything happens we don't expect," Jack went on, "we can just wing it."

Wing it. For somebody who liked to lay out her clothes the night before, plan menus by the month and schedule dental appointments a year in advance, those two words struck fear in Rachel's heart.

A bellhop strode to their car and welcomed them to the resort. Taking their luggage, he escorted them into the lobby. To Rachel's immense relief, somehow they managed to check in, get their key and make it to the fourth floor without running into anyone she knew.

So far, so good.

She wanted to get into their room, close the door, then survey the schedule they'd been given at the front desk for their group's activities over the next four days. With a little strategic planning, she and Jack could probably put in appearances here and there without actually having to interact in a significant way.

As they walked down the deserted hall toward their room, Rachel felt more at ease. Just the thought of planning made her feel calmer. Less anxious. More in control. Then Jack opened the door to their room, and her control flew right out the window.

It had a king-size bed, but she'd anticipated that. What she hadn't anticipated was the fireplace. The balcony. The wet bar. The canopy over the bed that made it look like something out of an Egyptian harem.

And mirrors. Everywhere there were mirrors.

"This has to be a mistake," she said. "I didn't book this room!"

"You didn't?"

"Of course not!"

She rushed into the bathroom and just about fainted. A whirlpool bathtub? A shower big enough for two? A bow-tied basket filled with massage oils? How could the hotel have screwed up like this? How? This was an environment made specifically for two people who wanted to do nothing but...

Oh.

Wait a minute.

She came out of the bathroom and saw Jack lounging casually on the sofa. Sure enough, there was the tiniest hint of a self-satisfied smirk on his face.

"You did this, didn't you?" she asked.

He blinked innocently. "Me? What makes you think it was me?"

"Are you denying it? Are you denying that you changed this reservation?"

He shrugged. "I just kind of...upgraded it a little."

"A *little?*" She looked at him with total disbelief. "When did you do it? Last night, after I went to bed?"

"I might have made a phone call."

"This is unbelievable."

"Hey, don't worry! I'm paying the difference. It won't cost Walter a dime."

"You *know* that's not the issue!"

"Then what is the issue?"

"The issue is that you're trying to...trying to—"

"Seduce you?" he said.

"Yes!"

"Uh...yeah. And your point is...?"

She glared at him, then threw her overnight bag down on the bed and followed it with her purse, the two of them clapping together. This was what she got for taking her eyes off him, even for five lousy minutes. He was a menace. That was what he was. She spun back around, intending to let him have it all over again.

Then she looked at the sofa.

Ha. He thought he was *so* smart.

She took a deep breath, let it out slowly, peace descending on her. She smiled sweetly. "Never mind, Jack. Thank you very much. I appreciate your getting this room. It's lovely."

Her looked at her warily.

"Yes. I'd forgotten. These suites really are deluxe. They come with a fireplace, a balcony, a whirlpool bathtub, and..." She gave him a smug smile. "A very comfortable sofa."

He sat up suddenly and looked down at the sofa, his own smile melting away.

"Which is where you'll be sleeping," she added.

"Now, wait a minute—"

"Sorry, Jack. You made your bed. Now you get to lie in it. *Alone*."

His look of distress lasted only a moment before he settled back on the sofa again. "That's okay."

"It is?"

"Sure. Just because we don't sleep together doesn't mean we can't do *other* things together."

"You're not getting this, Jack. When we're alone in here, I don't want you to touch me. I don't even want you to come near me."

He just smiled. She'd just told him he couldn't have what he came here for, and all he could do was smile? Did he think she was kidding about this?

"You're getting a free vacation here," she said. "The least you can do is agree to one simple ground rule."

"Actually that's a very complicated ground rule. Sharing a hotel room with you and not touching you..." He let out a sigh of misery. "God, Rachel. I'm a man. We don't do too well with restrictions like that."

"Sorry, you'll have to manage. When we're in this room, you have to promise me that you won't touch me."

He sighed again. "Sure. No problem."

"I don't believe you."

"You think I'm going to force myself on you? Is that what you think?"

"No, of course not. But—"

"If you say you don't want me to touch you when we're in here, then I won't."

"Good." She took a deep breath and let it out slowly. "I'm glad we understand each other."

"Of course we do. This has just become a no-touching zone."

"That's right."

"Are you planning on posting a warning sign?"

"Do you think that'll be necessary?"

He didn't respond. He merely smiled again, with a glint in his eyes that worried her. What was he thinking? Or plotting, to be more exact?

Rachel picked up the schedule. "Okay. Let's see. It says here that we're supposed to meet everyone for dinner tonight in the main dining room. We'll keep to ourselves as much as we can, then come back here as soon as we can. I want you to speak only when spoken to, and then as little as possible."

"Sounds like a real minimalist approach to a good time."

"We're not going there to have a good time."

"Then what are we going there for?"

"Because my boss expects us to be there."

"Oh. Does he also expect us to be miserable?"

Rachel closed her eyes. She couldn't believe this. Jack literally couldn't wait to jump right into the middle of things to see if he could continue to pass himself off as her husband, while she was already shaking in her boots at the very thought of saying hello.

Her husband. Handsome, smart, sexy—and a disaster waiting to happen.

AT RACHEL'S INSISTENCE, they stayed in their room the rest of the afternoon. Jack figured there was plenty of time left over the next four days to argue with her about that, so he settled onto the sofa and flipped on a ball game, while Rachel sat down at the desk, pulled folders out of a briefcase and appeared to be doing work from the office. He couldn't imagine that somebody would come to a ski resort and work, but her nose stayed to the grindstone for a good two hours.

Later they changed for dinner. Jack put on slacks and a sport coat. Rachel came out of the bathroom wearing a royal-blue dress that was amazingly sexy given the fact that the hem grazed her knees and the neckline went up to her chin. Exposure wasn't the key, so it must have been the fact that it hugged every curve, and Rachel had plenty of curves to hug.

She saw him staring. "What?"

"You look great."

"Jack—"

"Beautiful."

"Please don't—"

"Sexy."

She looked away.

"I'm guessing you don't take compliments very well," he told her. "Let me help you out. You're supposed to say, 'Thank you, Jack. You're looking pretty hot yourself.'"

She jerked her gaze around, and her cheeks came alive with color. God, he loved the way that happened every time he said something provocative, because it meant she could never fool him, never make him think she had no reaction at all to the things he said to her. Never.

She grabbed her purse. "It's time to go."

"So I guess I don't get a compliment after all?"

"You look very nice."

"Don't go overboard, now. You might embarrass me."

"I can't imagine a scenario under which you would be embarrassed, Jack. Not one."

Out of habit, he started to argue with her, only to realize that she was absolutely right.

A minute later they were in the elevator, descending toward the lobby. Rachel took a deep breath and let it out slowly.

"Okay. It's going to be like we talked about, right? If at all possible, you'll keep your mouth shut and let me field questions. And you won't leave my side at any time. For any reason."

"Any more rules you'd care to make?" Jack said.

"Yes. About a thousand more. They just haven't come to me yet."

"Can I go to the bathroom by myself?"

"As long as nobody I know is in there with you."

"Why don't you just come in with me and stand guard?"

"Don't push me. I just might."

He grinned. "Did I ever tell you about the fantasy I have about making love to a beautiful woman in a bathroom stall?"

Rachel stared at him dumbly, then closed her eyes and shook her head.

The elevator doors opened, and Jack took her arm. "Come on, sweetheart. It's showtime."

6

As they walked through the lobby toward the dining room, Rachel looked as if she was heading to her own execution. Her face was tight and drawn, those blue eyes of hers shifting nervously back and forth. She clutched her purse in her left hand, her right one closed in a tight fist. He reached down and took it, easing her fingers open and enveloping it in his.

"Wow," he said. "Your hand is freezing."

"Then why are you holding it?" she whispered.

"It needs warming up. And you look like you could use a little moral support."

"But you're the reason I *need* moral support."

"Then I guess I've got all the bases covered, don't I?"

Jack gave her another smile and squeezed her hand. She rolled her eyes a little, but she didn't pull away. That was a good sign. He might have to stick to the "no touching" rule in their room, but out here she was expected to act like his loving wife. And if it so happened that he was a particularly affectionate husband, wasn't that even better?

They reached the main dining room, which had been closed for their private party, and peered through the doorway. A dozen or so people were already milling around, holding drinks and chatting. The lights had been dimmed, leaving much of the illumination to candlelight, and linen-covered tables sparkled with silver and crystal.

"Rachel! Jack!"

At the sound of the booming voice, they turned to see Walter approaching, moving with all the subtlety of a typhoon rolling in.

"Haven't seen you two all afternoon!" he said, holding a martini glass that was nearly empty. "Didn't know if you'd made it in yet or not." He turned to Jack. "So. What do you think of this place? Pretty spectacular, isn't it?"

"Spectacular isn't the word for it," Jack said.

Rachel tightened her hand against his.

"Gotta tell you, Walter. When we came around the bend and I saw it for the first time, so big and shiny and sprawling out all over the landscape, well..."

Her fingernails dug into his palm.

"Well, I was speechless," Jack said. "Just speechless."

Walter beamed as if Jack had just declared the place to be the eighth wonder of the world. "Why thanks, Jack! That's pretty much everybody's reaction. Hey! Why don't you two join me and Emma at our table?"

Jack saw Rachel's eyes fly open wide. She moved her mouth to say something, but nothing came out. She clearly wanted to sit with anyone but Walter, but Jack knew the cardinal rule of office politics—one does not turn down an invitation from the boss.

"We'd love to," Jack said, and Rachel turned that deer-in-the-headlights expression right at him. As Walter escorted them to a table, she whispered to Jack.

"I don't believe this. Right off the bat we have to sit with Walter?"

"We don't have a choice."

"And your comment about the resort. Speechless? You were *speechless?* Was that the best you could do?"

"He took it as a compliment, didn't he?"

"If you were speechless," Rachel muttered, "it was only because you were gasping in horror."

When they'd almost reached the table, Rachel's eyes flew open wide again. "Oh, no."

"What?"

"Megan is there, too!"

"So?"

"She's a real gossip. If she even suspects something's up, we're in trouble."

Maybe that was true, but Jack knew it was always best to meet potential trouble head-on. He walked right up to her and stuck out his hand. "Hi, Megan. We met back at the office, remember?"

"Of course I remember," Megan said, shaking his hand. "Wish I could cook up birthday surprises that good for everybody else."

Megan was nice. Outgoing. A little goofy. One of those people Jack generally liked on sight. But he heeded Rachel's warning—she could very well be the sharpest person at the table and the most likely to pick up on anything that seemed out of place.

"Emma, sweetie," Walter said to another woman at the table, "this is Dr. Jack Kellerman, Rachel's husband. Jack, my wife, Emma."

Emma was a mousy little brown-haired woman, who said a quiet hello to go with her friendly smile as she shook Jack's hand. There was another couple at the table, who Walter introduced as Phil and Suzy Wardman. Phil, a senior architect at Davidson Design, was a slick-looking guy wearing a conservative navy suit and a big smile that seemed about as sincere as the average used car salesman's. Bleach-blond Suzy wore an equally phony smile and looked as if she spent all her time in shopping malls.

"About time we got to meet you," Phil said, shaking

Jack's hand a little too enthusiastically. "Where you been hiding this guy, Rachel? Huh?"

"He's a very busy man," Rachel said. "I'm just glad he could come along this weekend."

"Yeah," Phil said. "Isn't Walter a great guy for inviting everyone on this retreat?"

"He sure is," Suzy said, giving Walter a brilliant smile, then turning to Emma. "But I'm sure Emma had a hand in it, too."

Emma looked a little self-conscious. "Well, actually—"

"Don't be shy," Phil said. "Where would Walter be without his number one hostess?"

Oh, Lord. Jack had seen ass kissing in his day, but these two took the cake. Phil played yes-man, while Suzy was the consummate corporate wife, doting on Walter and Emma as if they were her long-lost grandparents. And by the way Walter's grin grew bigger with every breath, he was sucking up the compliments like a vacuum cleaner sucks up lint.

"Now, Jack," Suzy said, "why have we had to wait so long to meet you? We were beginning to think you didn't really exist."

Jack saw Rachel's eyes widen a little at that, but he knew that nobody had any clue that Suzy had just spoken the truth. Including Suzy.

"I'm afraid my schedule has been pretty hectic lately," Jack told her.

"Tell us about your South American operation," Walter said.

Jack could practically feel Rachel's anxiety level shoot through the roof. If she wasn't careful, she was going to be the one giving them away, not him.

"We're a group of doctors who fly to remote places to open medical clinics," Jack told Walter. "It's not just a matter of giving those people quality medical care. In some places, there's no medical care at all."

"That must take quite a lot of funding," Walter said.

"We have several private benefactors who are very generous."

"Apparently you spend quite a lot of time down there."

"Yes, the last several months in particular. We're in the process of opening up a new clinic fifty miles or so outside of Bogotá. Rachel has been really understanding about me being gone for weeks on end, so whenever I get back to the States..." He turned and gave her an adoring look. "Well, let's just say that by the time we spend all the private time together we want to, it's time for me to fly off again. That's why I haven't had the chance yet to meet all of you."

Rachel smiled at him. It was a little shaky, but it *was* a smile.

"So what made you take up that particular cause?" Walter asked.

"An old college buddy of mine was part of the group, and when he told me about it, suddenly my white-coat practice didn't seem so meaningful anymore."

"Are you a surgeon?" Suzy asked.

"Family practice," Rachel said.

"Oh," Suzy said, with an indulgent smile. "How nice."

Apparently Rachel's choice of phony specialty for him didn't live up to Suzy's standards. Megan rolled her eyes in Suzy's general direction. Jack felt like doing a little eye-rolling of his own.

"Are you still practicing medicine in the States?" Walter asked.

"No. The clinics are a full-time effort for me."

Suzy's eyes widened. "You mean you gave up a medical practice in the United States to take care of people in the backwoods of Columbia? Sounds rather...barbaric."

For a woman who probably couldn't comprehend life without hairdressers and shopping malls, the mere thought of performing altruistic missions for less fortunate people clearly didn't compute.

Jack leaned toward her, capturing her gaze with his. "You know, Suzy, I understand exactly what you're saying. I was inclined to think that, too, in the beginning. Then one week I hopped a plane with my friend and went down there, and I've got to tell you, it changed my life."

By the way Suzy was staring at him, he knew he had her on the hook.

"Imagine a place in the world," he said, "where few have known the luxury of electricity and running water. Where having food on the table every day is nothing more than a dream. Where babies are stillborn because their mothers are malnourished. Where children often die before the age of five because their parents haven't even heard of immunizations. Imagine that, and you'll know why it's so important for somebody to go down there and make their lives better."

Suzy blinked. "Oh. Well. Of course. I didn't mean that somebody shouldn't do something. You know. Somebody."

"Somebody like Jack?" Megan said.

Suzy's face creaked open just a little, finally emitting the tiniest little ray of approval. "Yes. His effort on behalf of those poor people is very...impressive."

"Poor is right," Megan said, "Can you even imagine a place where people drive ox carts instead of Beemers?"

Suzy shot Megan a subtle look of pure contempt, and Megan pretended not to notice.

"But I'm sure you're involved in plenty of volunteer efforts of your own," Jack said to Suzy.

"Of course she is," Phil said.

Suzy whipped around to look at her husband, her eyes wide.

"She went with some of the women from our neighborhood association and manned telephones during the public television pledge drive last year."

"Really?" Jack said, interjecting just the right amount of awe into his voice, which was pretty much none at all.

"Oh, yeah," Phil went on. "And she always gives all of her clothes from last season to charity." He turned to Suzy. "Oh! And remember when you were in college, and your sorority served Thanksgiving dinner at that homeless shelter?"

Suzy gave him a nervous little smile of agreement, then took a heavy swig of her chardonnay.

The more Jack got a handle on the dynamics of this particular group, the more he realized that Rachel had nothing to worry about. Phil couldn't see beyond his own brown nose. Suzy spent all her time trying to keep the silver spoon in her mouth. Emma couldn't have cared less who was married and who wasn't. Megan liked him too much to dig for a whole lot of dirt, and any suspicion Walter might accidentally develop could be stopped dead in its tracks by tossing a bone to his hungry ego.

On that last note, Jack settled back in his chair, then turned to Walter. "Tell me more about this resort. You've got a lot to be proud of here. As I said, it just leaves me speechless."

RACHEL COULDN'T BELIEVE IT. They were actually pulling this off.

The main course came and went, then dessert, and soon

they were sipping after-dinner drinks, and not one person seemed inclined to stand up, point a finger at Jack and declare him to be an impostor.

The most astonishing thing of all, though, was Jack's ability to turn the conversation around until he wasn't answering questions, but asking them. And since most people were more than happy to talk about themselves, once the initial exchange when they sat down at the table was done, nobody asked Jack a single question about his work in South America. Instead he discussed gardening with Emma, grunge bands with Megan, and soon he had Suzy eating out of his hand by telling her how important her work with public television was, and how he couldn't imagine life without it. Even Phil warmed up to him a little when Jack hung on every word he spoke about his painfully limited college football career.

But just as Rachel thought they were going to get through the entire evening with their deception intact, during a lull in the conversation, Megan turned to her and said, "So, tell me. How did you and Jack meet?"

Rachel froze. How did they meet?

Oh, God. There it was. Something they hadn't covered. She couldn't believe what a fool she was. Of course somebody could ask that. Why hadn't she been prepared?

Everyone at the table fell silent, waiting for the answer to Megan's question. Rachel turned to Jack, her eyes wide. She'd never been good at off-the-cuff responses. She had an incredible memory, but she had to put something there in the first place to eventually remember it. And right now, nothing was coming to her. Absolutely nothing.

Then Jack slid his hand over hers and gave her a warm smile. "At the Alamo."

Rachel blinked with surprise. The truth? She never would have thought of that.

"The Alamo?" Phil said. "You mean that place where everybody died?"

"Yes," Jack said, turning to stare at Rachel. "See, I'm kind of a history buff, so when I lived in San Antonio, sometimes I went to the Alamo just to look around. Then one day, there she was."

The women around the table had leaned in closer, not because the Alamo was such a scintillating topic, but because Jack's voice had slid down into a lower register, smooth and warm and very, very sexy.

"Behind the chapel at the Alamo," Jack went on, his gaze never leaving hers, "there's an old well. She was standing next to it, reading the inscription, and I swear I thought an angel had flown to earth. It was a hot summer day, and her hair..."

He slipped the back of his hand beneath the dark strands, lifted them slightly, then let it fall in ripples against her shoulder.

"...her hair shimmered in the sunlight."

Rachel swallowed hard, realizing that all movement around the table had ceased. Everyone's eyes were on Jack, and Jack's eyes were on her.

"I walked over and stood beside her," he went on. "She turned. Slowly she took her sunglasses off, and I saw her eyes for the first time. Ice-blue eyes, right there in the dead of summer, the most beautiful eyes I'd ever seen. Then she smiled, and I was a goner. Totally, completely gone. And I haven't come back since."

He leaned in close and pressed a gentle kiss to her lips. Rachel's heart hammered in her chest. He'd spoken the truth, at least about where they were when they met. But how he'd felt at that moment—was he also telling the truth about that?

No. Of course not. Jack was nothing if not dramatic, and

if he wasn't careful, these people were going to know he was embellishing.

Then Rachel glanced at Suzy. She had her elbow resting on the table, her chin in her hand, staring at Jack dreamily.

"That is *so* romantic," she said.

Suddenly she jumped a little and faced her husband, her brows drawn together in a tight frown. Phil had clearly nudged her under the table. Hard.

"That's a lovely story," Emma said. "Walter and I met when he rear-ended my car on Colfax Avenue."

"Hey, that was no accident," Walter said with a big grin. "I saw her and I had to have her. How else was I supposed to get her to stop?"

"You were changing the radio station in your car and didn't see me stop in front of you."

Everybody laughed. Emma smiled, and Walter gave her a quick peck on the lips. "Hey, I was trying my best to catch up to Jack in the romance department, and you had to go and tell the truth."

Everybody laughed again, and the conversation took off in yet another direction. But just as Rachel started to relax again, Jack rested his hand against her thigh under the table.

She tried not to react, but his touch was like an electric shock. She shifted a little, which only made the hem of her dress shift higher, which Jack followed with his hand. At the same time he was talking to everyone else at the table, he began a slow, mesmerizing motion with his thumb, moving it in tiny little circles. Rachel was shocked at the way her blood seemed to heat up at just that simple touch.

She leaned in and whispered in Jack's ear. "What about my rule?"

"Rule?" he whispered back.

"About touching."

"We're not in our room, are we?"

"It goes for here, too."

"Sorry. The game's already started. You can't change the rules."

"But—"

He kissed her.

"Jack—"

He kissed her again, then leaned in and whispered, "I'm playing the part of your husband, remember?"

"There's such a thing as overacting."

"Maybe the other men here tonight are underacting."

Rachel glanced quickly across the table at Suzy and found her staring, a touch of longing in her eyes. Then Suzy looked over at her own husband. Phil's attention was focused on one thing only: trying to get everyone's attention focused on him. And for the first time, Rachel realized just how unhappy Suzy appeared to be about that.

A slow crescendo of understanding unfurled inside her. As Jack had talked about the moment they met, she was sure that he'd overdone it, sure that everyone saw through him, that they were thinking to themselves, Who is this guy?

Now she realized that was exactly what they were thinking. Who is this guy who pays so much attention to his wife? Who looks at her as if he's seeing her for the first time? Who can't seem to wait until he gets her back to their room and between the sheets?

Maybe she wasn't the focus of suspicion after all. Maybe she was the focus of...jealousy?

A warm glow started in the pit of Rachel's stomach and radiated through her whole body. For a moment, she succumbed to Jack's charms herself, caught in the spell of his voice, his eyes, his words, the warm feeling of his hand against her thigh, and for a moment, she almost believed that they really were married and she really was the love of his life.

Then she remembered why he was really here. He wanted a no-cost, sex-filled, four-day vacation. He was trying to seduce her. Hadn't he admitted it point-blank? She was nothing more than a challenge to him. Maybe she was the first woman who'd ever disappeared in the middle of the night, and his ego couldn't take the rejection. That's why he was here now. To get back on top, figuratively speaking. And once he did, she had a feeling that his preoccupation with her would dim considerably.

Jack finally did as she asked and took his hand away from her thigh, only to drape it across the back of her chair and perform the same maddening movement of his thumb on her upper arm. Even with the fabric of her dress to keep them from skin-to-skin contact, she felt every motion of his thumb as if she weren't wearing anything at all.

After another half hour, people started checking watches, and finally everyone rose to leave.

"Phil, Rachel, Megan," Walter said, "I'll see the three of you in the Redwood Room at nine o'clock tomorrow for the employee meeting. The speaker I have coming has agreed to do a three-hour program instead of two. I think you'll find it fascinating."

Rachel froze. Three hours? Three hours during which she'd be one place, and Jack would be another? The very thought of that struck fear in her heart.

Then Suzy sidled up next to Jack. "Several of us are going skiing while our spouses are in that meeting. You'll come with us, won't you?"

"Skiing?" he said.

"Yes, Jack," Emma said. "Please join us."

"I'd love to," he said.

Rachel's heart stood still. Had he actually said he'd go?

She couldn't believe it. He could have talked his way out of that so easily. Why hadn't he?

"We're meeting in the lobby at nine o'clock tomorrow morning," Suzy told him.

"Great," Jack said. "I'll see you then."

She and Jack left the dining room and headed for the elevators. "Why did you tell Emma and Suzy that you'd go skiing with them?" Rachel whispered.

"Uh...because I like to ski?"

"Didn't I tell you that you need to lie low?"

"It won't be a problem. Trust me."

"It gives them that much more chance to ask you questions you can't answer!"

"They won't be doing that. They've got no reason to. We'll be skiing. That's all."

"Jack, you promised. You promised you wouldn't go anywhere without me."

He punched the button for the elevator. "No, I believe that was a rule you made. One I never actually agreed to."

She bowed her head. Why did he have to make things so difficult? Why?

She didn't speak to him all the way up the elevator. Once they were in their room, Jack hung up his coat in the closet, then turned to face her.

"I don't understand what's bothering you. Didn't things go well tonight?"

"Yes," she admitted, tossing her purse down on the dresser. "They did. Well, except for when Megan asked how we met."

"What was wrong with that?"

"You laid it on so thick that I was afraid nobody was going to buy it."

"What are you talking about?"

"All that 'hair shimmering in the sunlight, ice-blue

eyes' stuff. I mean, come on, Jack. That was so unbelievable."

"Why was it unbelievable?"

"Because husbands don't talk about their wives like that, that's why."

"They don't?"

"No."

"Why not?"

She blinked. "I don't know why. They just don't."

"Didn't your parents talk about each other like that?"

"Oh, good God, no."

"Did they love each other?"

She paused. "Sure. Of course they did. They just had a very civil marriage."

"Civil?"

Rachel kicked off her shoes. "They respected each other."

"Sounds like a real bore."

"They were very compatible."

"You mean they bored each other."

"Their relationship was very...strong."

"In or out of the bedroom?"

"Now, how in the world would I know that?"

"Oh, you know. Believe me, you know."

She did. Not once in her life had she ever been able to imagine that her parents did anything in the bedroom except sleep, because she could barely recall them even touching when they were outside the bedroom. And she had to think that that kind of icy behavior had to translate to between the sheets, too.

"Hey," Jack said, "aren't you ever afraid that your parents will come to Denver and wonder why their daughter got married without telling them?"

"They won't come to Denver."

"Why not? Don't they ever visit?"

"No. I go back to the East Coast a couple of times a year."

"Ah. The old Thanksgiving and Christmas visits. The obligatory ones."

Actually that was exactly what they were. Even though she'd been the one to do everything her parents approved of, still she felt nothing but disapproval the entire time she was with them. Then, if her sister actually happened to grace everyone with her presence, the entire experience could turn positively arctic. Those two visits were generally a strong enough dose of family to last her the rest of the year.

"Never mind all that," Rachel said. "From now on, when you're talking about us, you really need to tone it down. I mean, do you really think that anyone there tonight believed that the moment we met, the world actually stopped spinning on its axis?"

He took two steps toward her, closing the distance between them. He stared down at her, his incredible green eyes fixed relentlessly on hers.

"Yes," he said. "I think they believed every word."

"Oh? Why do you say that?"

"Because it's the truth."

7

Rachel froze, staring at Jack, looking for that ever-present twinkle in his eyes that said he was making yet one more joke. For once, it was strangely absent. Instead he looked at her intensely, knowingly, as if he meant every word he said.

The very thought that he'd been serious, that the moment they met had been as exhilarating for him as he'd described it at the dinner table tonight, made her breath catch in her throat. She tried to act nonchalant, but that was a very hard thing to do when Jack's gaze slid from her face to her neck, then lower to her breasts, where it lingered for a moment before coming back up. She froze, her heart hammering in her chest, feeling as if the world had halted a second time and was hovering in place, waiting for him to reach out and—

"This has been a really long day," he said. "I think I'll hit the sack."

Huh?

He fished through one of the dresser drawers and pulled out a pair of pajama bottoms. "Mind if I have the bathroom first? Don't mean to malign women as a whole, but on the average they do tend to take a while, and I'd like to get in, get out, and get to sleep."

"Uh...yeah. Sure."

He went into the bathroom and closed the door behind him. Rachel stared dumbly at the door for a moment, then turned and collapsed on the bed, every nerve ending still alive and tingling. For a moment there, she'd been absolutely sure that he intended to...

No. Of course he didn't intend to touch her at all. Not in this room, anyway. Apparently he was finally respecting her wishes. That was a good thing. A very good thing.

Wasn't it?

A few minutes later he came out of the bathroom, wearing the pajama bottoms. Nothing else. Bare feet, bare arms, bare chest. And what a gorgeous chest it was, with just the right amount of muscle definition and golden hair sprinkled in just the right places. And those beautiful broad shoulders—there was something so *right* about those, too, that she just couldn't help staring...

Staring. She was staring.

She looked away quickly, but not before he saw her looking at him, and...

Oh, hell.

She grabbed her robe and nightgown, then slipped past him and went into the bathroom. She shut the door and leaned against it, her eyes closed. Good *Lord*. Here she was getting all fluttery at the sight of Jack's half-naked body, and there weren't even any power tools in sight.

She did her business, then put on a nightgown with her blue robe over it. When she came out, Jack was lying on a pillow bunched against the arm of the sofa, a blanket pulled up to his waist, his chest still bare. She averted her gaze, resisting the urge to scream at him: *It's winter, for heaven's sake! Would you kindly put on a shirt?*

"Meant to tell you back at your house," he said. "Sexy robe you've got there."

She strode to the king-size bed. "Sorry I'm not dressing to thrill you."

"Undressing. That's what would thrill me."

"Sorry. I'm not going to do that, either."

"Oh, well. Can't blame a guy for trying."

She blinked with surprise. He called that trying? This was not like Jack. Not in the least.

"Mind getting the light?" he said.

She turned off the lamp, then removed her robe, tossing it on the foot of the bed. She climbed beneath the covers and settled her head against the pillow, staring into the darkness of the room.

"Jack?"

"Yeah?"

"I can't believe you're actually living up to our agreement."

"What agreement is that?"

"No touching while we're in this room."

"Oh, that. You sound surprised."

"Flabbergasted is more like it."

"I told you I wouldn't touch you when we're in here, and I meant it. Though I must say that it *is* a waste of a perfectly good king-size bed. Not to mention the whirlpool tub." He sighed dramatically. "But rules are rules."

"Yes. They are. And actually, those things won't go to waste at all. This bed is quite comfortable, and I intend to float around in the hot tub for a while tomorrow, too."

"Naked?"

"Is there any other way?"

"Alone?"

"I believe I made that clear."

"Because I can't touch you."

"That's right."

Rachel pulled the covers up closer to her neck, and for a long time she heard nothing but the soft rumble of the elevator down the hall. But just when she felt certain he must have fallen asleep, she heard his voice again across the darkened room.

"Well, then. If I can't touch you, then I guess you'll have to do it for me."

Rachel froze. "What?"

"Touch your breasts," he murmured. "Tell me what they feel like."

Rachel gasped. *"What?"*

"Shall I repeat it?"

"No!"

"Never mind. I'm pretty sure I can remember on my own." He paused, his words slipping out on a soft breath. "Oh, yeah. I remember, all right."

"Jack—"

"First I remember opening the door to that hotel room in San Antonio. I could barely get the key in the lock because you were telling me to hurry."

Embarrassment shot through her at the memory of her desperate plea for him to open the door, because no matter how much she wanted him, some still-sane part of her had told her it just wouldn't be right to rip his clothes off out there in the hallway.

"Then we got into the room, slammed the door behind us and I kissed you. Backed straight up against the door and kissed you, long and hard."

Rachel could barely breathe when she thought about that. After all, hadn't she played that moment over in her mind at least a million times?

"Then you wrapped your arms around my neck," he went on. "I kept on kissing you. Then I put my hand against your waist and eased it up until I was touching your breast. It felt so good to touch you like that...so *good*...and I thought, she's *perfect*. I thought I'd died and gone to heaven."

She wanted to tell him to stop, firmly and with no equivocation. But for some unfathomable reason, the words just wouldn't come out of her mouth.

"Then I ran my fingertips over your breast," he said. "Even through your shirt and your bra, I could feel that your nipple was already hard. Tight. You moaned just a little, then leaned into me, kissing me even deeper, and I remember thinking, *yes*. After being together all day, dying to touch you like that, I was finally doing it, and you were loving it. I swear, Rachel, I just about lost it right there."

She had, too. She couldn't remember ever wanting any man the way she'd wanted Jack at that moment.

"Tell me," he whispered. "Are your nipples hard now?"

Her heart jolted.

"Touch them," he said.

This was crazy. Absolutely crazy. Did he actually think she would—

"It's dark in here," he murmured. "You're under the covers. I'll never know if you're really touching them or not." He paused. "But believe me, either way I'm going to imagine that you are."

His words were like little electric shocks zinging her from across the room, making every nerve in her body tense with anticipation. She knew somehow that she should feel embarrassed. Or offended. Instead she felt...excited.

She knew what he was doing. Even if he couldn't touch her, he was still trying to get to her, to make her want him right *now*, and damned if it wasn't working.

Slowly she brought her hands up beneath the covers, careful not to cause a ripple on the surface. She touched her breasts, sliding her thumbs across her nipples.

"How do they feel, Rachel? Are they hard? Tight?"

Yes!

The word came so clearly into her mind she was afraid for a moment that she'd spoken it out loud. But she hadn't. He had no way of knowing what she was doing, no way of knowing for sure that she was listening, that every word he spoke made her body hum with excitement.

"Don't stop," he whispered. "Keep touching them."

His voice was low and compelling. Hypnotic. This was insane. To be lying here doing this... What was she thinking?

She was thinking that she hadn't felt this excited in months. Six months, to be exact.

"Close your eyes," Jack whispered.

She let her eyes drift closed.

"Now," he murmured, "imagine that I'm the one touching you."

Thinking about the two of them in that San Antonio hotel room made every nerve in her body leap with sheer, hot energy. She was straddling his hips, her breasts thrust forward, her eyes closed, as he caressed her endlessly, his thumbs strumming her nipples. The image was so real that for a moment she was transported back in time, feeling his hands, hearing his voice, thinking that she'd never been with a man who'd made her feel so shockingly sensual in all her life.

"Think about how it felt when I touched you. Imagine that your hands are my hands. Do you feel them?"

Her heart hammered her chest. She hoped he couldn't hear her breathing, because it was coming faster now, in short, sharp intakes that she had to fight to keep silent.

"Are you hot?" he whispered.

Yes. Inside and out. So hot she wanted to rip the blankets off. So hot she wanted to leap out of this bed, yank the covers off him and drag him right up next to her. Drag him right *inside* her.

"Are you wet?"

Her heart jolted again.

"Are you, Rachel?"

Was she?

She squeezed her eyes closed, knowing she should turn away, put her hands over her ears, do anything to block out his mesmerizing voice, because she was rapidly losing what little bit of self-control she had left.

"I'd touch you if I could," he murmured. "I'd find out for myself. Unfortunately, I'm afraid your rule says I can't." He paused. "But you can. Do it, Rachel."

It wasn't a taunt. It was almost...a plea.

For a long time she heard nothing except the blood pumping through her head and echoing in her ears, feeling as if she'd stepped outside her own body and was watching every erotic moment unfold.

He won't know. He has no way of knowing...

Slowly she eased her nightgown up, careful not to disturb the covers, then parted her legs slightly and slipped her hand beneath her panties. She nearly gasped. She was hot and wet and hypersensitive, the tiniest touch sending ripples of heat radiating though her entire body.

"Now imagine it's me touching you there," he said.

In her mind, she saw him. In her touch, she felt him. With her eyes closed, with his voice carrying her away, suddenly he seemed to be everywhere at once. She imagined his body joining with hers in a hard, hot, satisfying rhythm that made them both crazy with desire.

"Imagine that I'm touching you," he repeated, his voice low and silky smooth. "Slowly. Deeply. I've done it before, Rachel. Remember? Imagine that I'm doing it again. Just...imagine."

She did. Seconds passed. A minute. Then two. She played his words over and over in her mind, letting them choreograph every move she made, and soon, very soon, she was actually on the verge of...

She couldn't believe it. Her heart was pounding, and her mouth felt dry as parchment. She felt as if she was climbing a mountain peak, knowing all the while that she was only seconds away from being pushed over the edge. She waited for his voice to drift across the darkness again, to send her higher...higher...

Jack? Are you there?

Silence.

She lay motionless, waiting. And waiting.

And waiting.

Say something!

Nothing.

She pulled her hand back, slowly, quietly, trying desperately to breathe without making a sound. After several more minutes of silence, during which she was sure she was going to internally combust, finally she couldn't stand it any longer.

"Jack?" she whispered.

"So you are awake."

She felt a surge of embarrassment, but it disappeared almost immediately. The fact that she'd spoken his name told him for sure that she'd been listening to him, tuning in to every word he spoke, but she didn't care. All she cared about was the way he was making her feel—crazy with lust, crazy with need. Just plain *crazy*.

"I'm still thinking about you," he said.

Tendrils of sheer, hot longing wrapped themselves around her, refusing to let go. She wanted him. Right now. But she couldn't say it. She couldn't. That would be playing right into his hands. Right into his arms, to be more precise.

But...would it really be so wrong? If she begged him to come over here, to climb beneath the covers with her and finish with his body what he'd started with his words, in just a few minutes both of them could be—

"And in a moment," he said, "I'll be dreaming about you."

Rachel froze. Sleep? He was going to sleep? While she was going nuts, he was going to *sleep?*

"Good night, Rachel."

She heard him shift on the sofa, and a soft *shush* of blankets skimming along his body. Then he was still.

For at least ten minutes, she didn't move. It took that long for her heart to stop pounding and for her breathing to return to normal.

Was he actually asleep? She didn't know.

She wanted to call out his name. *Scream* his name. Beg him to come to her right now.

Damned rule.

No. Keeping Jack at arm's length was the right thing to do. This man was clearly an expert at seduction—hadn't she fallen for him in a heartbeat that day in San Antonio? Every word he'd spoken then had been calculated to make her crazy with desire, just as the words he'd spoken tonight were meant to do.

She just didn't understand it. She had no trouble controlling herself in every other situation of her life, but the moment Jack touched her, kissed her—the moment he *spoke*—she couldn't think straight. In her carefully constructed world where she had complete control of everything, he made her feel as if she had no control at all.

And she knew that he was aware of that fact. He knew

she'd been listening to his every word, that he was doing more to excite her sexually from across the room than any other man had ever been able to do with skin-to-skin contact. He *knew* it.

Well, he wasn't going to know it anymore.

No matter what she had to do, she wasn't going to let him knock her off balance again, hitting her with things she wasn't expecting so she wouldn't know how to react. Too much was at stake this weekend for her to get distracted like that. She decided that from now on, the minute he opened his mouth again and that rich, sinful baritone came floating out, she was going to stop him cold, no matter what she had to do.

Okay, that was going to be easier said than done. But it *was* going to be done.

Her conviction firmly in place, she closed her eyes to sleep. The moment she did, though, she saw Jack's face, felt his hands, heard his voice, and she knew beyond a shadow of a doubt that before the night was over, she'd be dreaming about him, too.

JACK LAY ON THE SOFA, staring into the darkness of the room, on the verge of leaping up and doing one of two things: jumping into bed with Rachel and making wild, hot love to her all night long, or taking a shower—a shower so cold it would freeze the fur right off a polar bear. Since he couldn't do the former, the latter was really becoming something to consider.

Just imagining her touching herself had been enough to nearly send him right over the edge. With every word he'd spoken, he'd pictured being in bed with her, touching her just as he'd described, adding in some deep, prolonged kisses with their tongues intertwined, then pressing her to her back, her dark hair spread out on the pillow.

He'd move on top of her as she looked up at him with a heavy-lidded, pleading expression, wanting him, *needing* him...

For a moment while he'd been talking to her, he was afraid she'd fallen asleep. Then she'd called out his name, and he'd just about forgotten his promise and jumped right into her bed. And that would have been a hell of a bad move. Even if she'd given in tonight, he had a feeling that tomorrow morning she'd have run scared all over again.

He had to stick to her rule, no matter how stupid he thought it was. But that didn't mean he couldn't sidestep the rule, twist the rule and bend the rule every waking moment they were in here, forcing her to remember just how incredible things had been between them. But when it came to actually *breaking* the rule...

That, he decided, would have to be up to Rachel.

THE NEXT MORNING, RACHEL spent three hours in a hotel ballroom "interacting" with her co-workers and doing "team building" exercises led by some guy who'd written a book on the subject of corporate employee relations. Of course, Walter loved all that touchy-feely stuff, so he held this particular speaker in high esteem, while Rachel thought the guy's exorbitant fee was better than a license to steal.

But even if the activities had been positively scintillating, Rachel couldn't have participated with enthusiasm if her life depended on it. The only thing she could think about was how Jack was in the company of those women this morning, any one of whom could trip him up when he wasn't prepared.

Actually, that wasn't *all* she could think about.

Every time her mind started to wander, she heard Jack

talking to her, his words from last night drifting through her mind on clouds of sheer lust. During the lecture part of the presentation, she tried to take organized and systematic notes as she always did, only to realize that she was drawing little suns and moons and stars in the margins of her paper in a mindless little planetarium show.

This was bad. She was becoming a doodler. A *cosmic* doodler, at that. There was probably something symbolic in there somewhere, but she knew if she went so far as to actually analyze it, it would only prove that she really was a goner.

This morning before she and Jack went to breakfast, she'd started to tell him for the umpteenth time to watch every word that came out of his mouth, but she found it hard even to look him in the eye after what had happened. And all during the meal, he'd stared at her in a way that said he knew she'd been listening to him last night, doing every shameless thing he told her to.

The minute the meeting broke up, Rachel headed to the lobby and found Emma and Suzy and a couple of the other women Jack had been with. They told her he'd gone up to their room. She searched their faces for one of those "I know some gossip, and boy, is it juicy" looks that would have made her die right on the spot, but fortunately she saw nothing like that. They all merely remarked on what a wonderful skier her husband was, and how delighted they'd been that he could come along.

Rachel went up the elevator, trying to calm down. Things appeared to have gone well, but until she saw Jack and got a play-by-play of what had happened on the slopes this morning, her nerves were going to stay in knots.

She came into their room to find him crashed on the sofa, wearing jeans and a burgundy cotton sweater over a

T-shirt. He had his head propped on a pillow, watching CNN.

"How did it go?" she asked.

He sat up and stretched a little. "I had a great time. The sun was out, the snow was perfect—"

"You *know* what I mean."

"You mean, did I slip up and say something stupid so now everyone knows that I'm not really your husband?"

"Yes!"

He pondered that for a moment with an intense look of concentration on his face. Then he flipped off the TV and tossed the remote aside. "No, I don't believe I remember saying anything like that."

She wanted to scream. She'd been worried like crazy for the past three hours, and he was making light of her fears. Didn't he get it? Didn't he understand that every word out of his mouth was a potential time bomb?

He could have slipped up and not known it. He could have acted suspiciously, and only now was somebody catching on. Maybe somewhere in one of these rooms right now, some woman was saying to her husband, *You know, that Jack Kellerman? Something's awfully fishy about that man...*

"Are you absolutely sure you didn't say something to get me into trouble?"

"Yes. I'm sure."

"So what happened on the slopes?"

"We skied."

"What else?"

"Nothing."

"Tell me what you talked about."

"Nothing of any consequence."

"Are you *sure* you didn't say anything wrong?"

"Yes, Rachel. I'm sure."

"Not even something tiny? Something that seemed insignificant when you said it, but really wasn't?"

"I told you," he said with exasperation. "Nothing happened."

"You're sure?"

He opened his mouth to protest again, then shut it. A moment later, his eyebrows quirked up. "Well, there was that one little thing..."

"Oh, God," she breathed, sliding her hand up to her throat. "What?"

"Well, it started out when Emma was complaining that Walter was having trouble...uh...performing in bed."

"She *what?*"

"Yeah. And then she asked for my advice."

"Asked for your *advice?* Emma Davidson? About... about Walter? About their *sex life?*"

"She wanted to know if I thought it would help if she greeted him at the door at night wearing sexy lingerie."

"She did not ask you that!"

"I told her to forget the sexy lingerie. That it would be better if she were stark naked."

Rachel's mouth fell open. "You didn't!"

"Oh, yeah. And then she asked me if you'd ever greeted me at the door wearing nothing at all."

Rachel gasped with horror.

"I told her that was silly. That of course you were wearing something."

She let out a breath of relief.

"A little heart tattoo on your left hip that you got the last time we were in New Orleans."

She gasped again. "*What?* I haven't got a tattoo! Why would you tell her that? Jack! That woman is my boss's wife!" She sank to the sofa and buried her head in her hands. "Tell me you didn't actually tell her I have a tattoo," she pleaded. "And that I came to the door *naked*. Please tell me—"

"Of course I didn't. But since you were absolutely certain that I must have said something really awful, I figured I'd better not disappoint you."

She snapped her head up, her heart still hammering in her chest. "Are you telling me you made all that *up*?"

"Well, I did go skiing. That part was true. But I'm afraid I don't know a thing about Emma and Walter's sex life."

"You lied to me?"

"Hey, I tried the truth," he said. "You didn't want that."

Rachel just stared at him, absolutely speechless.

"When I tell you everything's fine, you can believe it. I have no intention of saying anything that's going to get you into trouble. Will you just trust me on that?"

She wanted desperately to be mad, but she *had* pushed him. Hard. And now he was smiling at her again, and...

She sighed. "I guess I'm just worried, you know? I'm worried that—"

"Okay. There's your problem. You worry too much."

"Would you tell me just exactly how I'm supposed to *stop* worrying?"

He smiled. "Simple. Stop focusing on what could go wrong, and start focusing on having a good time. For instance, where do you want to go to lunch?"

Lunch? She'd just about had heart failure. The last thing she wanted to do was eat.

"I'm not hungry."

"Sure you are. It's almost one o'clock."

She let out a weary breath. "Fine. We'll order room service."

"Room service? We're here at this stunning resort, and you want to stay in the room? Let's go out."

"No. Wherever we go around here, I'll see people I work with."

"So? We still have three days here. We'll have to see them sometime."

"I know. Just not now."

"Then let's find a restaurant outside the resort."

"I said I want to stay in the room."

"A nice, out-of-the-way place where nobody will know us. And I'll buy."

"No. We're getting room service. Period."

He raised an eyebrow and stared at her skeptically. "Rachel? What are you up to?"

"What?"

"You wouldn't be trying to...seduce me, would you?"

She sat up straight. "*Seduce* you?"

"Don't play dumb with me. I see what you're doing. You're planning on ordering a nice lunch for just the two of us, and maybe a bottle of wine, which you'll want to drink in the bathtub. Naked, of course."

"I don't want to do any such thing!"

"And pretty soon we'll be sprawled out on the bed, feeding each other grapes. No, wait. Strawberries. *Chocolate-dipped* strawberries. That's what you have in mind, isn't it?"

"Absolutely not!"

"One thing will lead to another, and before I know it you'll be on the phone, asking room service if they'll bring us a can of whipped cream, which you'll then proceed to squirt all over your—"

"Oh, all right!" she shouted. "We'll go out!"

He drew back with a startled look. "Well, okay. We can go out. If you really feel that strongly about it."

She looked at him with utter disbelief. She'd never met anyone in her life who could manipulate a situation the way this man could, who got what he wanted using nothing but verbal gymnastics and sheer persistence. What had she done to deserve this? What?

Nothing. Well, almost nothing. She *had* told a tiny little fib that just happened to get big.

So what now? She could go out in public and risk dealing with her co-workers, or stay in this room and risk dealing with Jack. Thinking about the look she'd seen in his eyes when he talked about whipped cream, she decided maybe a public place wasn't that risky after all.

"Why don't I call the concierge?" Jack said. "Get a recommendation? A quiet, quaint place with at least one salad on the menu. How does that sound?"

It sounded as if she was heading for big trouble. This was a bad idea. She could feel it in her bones. It appeared that she'd lucked out so far today and her secret was still a secret. But how many more chances could she take before her luck ran out?

"I need aspirin," Rachel said, heading toward the bathroom.

"This is going to be fun," he called after her as he picked up the phone. "You'll see."

As if that was supposed to calm her fears. A crazy man telling her something was going to be fun.

Oh, yeah. She felt better already.

8

WHEN THEY LEFT THE HOTEL, Rachel headed toward her car, but Jack grabbed her arm and directed her to a cab instead. He wanted her to be comfortable. Loosen up a little. Maybe have a drink or two. If she drove, she couldn't do any of those things.

As they made their way into Silver Springs, Rachel slowly started coming to life. It turned out that the restaurant sat one block off the main drag that ran through the center of town, where old shops had been renovated to reflect their nineteenth-century origins. She tried to hide it, but he could see her eyes light up with interest as they passed a drugstore, a lounge, a hotel, an opera house, a church—all steeped in the architecture of the late-nineteenth century. But she wasn't saying a word. Apparently she knew that if she pointed out how warm and historic this little town was, she'd be maligning the company she worked for, then maligning herself for the part she'd had in blighting the landscape with that monstrosity of a resort.

The driver turned off Main Street and pulled up in front of the restaurant, a cheery little neighborhood bar and grill housed between a feed store and a real estate office. Jack paid the driver, then slid out of the cab and held the door open for Rachel. As she stepped out, the wind caught her dark hair and swirled it around her head, and within seconds her cheeks were tinted pink from the cold.

She looked beautiful, even without the smile he was hell-bent on putting back onto her face.

Then halfway to the door of the restaurant, she stopped suddenly.

"What?" he asked.

"Are you out of your mind? I'm not going in there!"

"Why not?"

"Because it's so loud in there that I can hear the music out here!"

"Good. If we get rowdy, it won't be a problem."

Rachel gave him a look that said the word *rowdy* wasn't even in her vocabulary. She tiptoed closer and peered through the window. "And look at that decor! It's awful!"

"I don't plan on eating the artwork."

"The waitresses are practically falling out of their T-shirts."

Jack looked through the window, then grinned. "Why, look at that. They sure are."

She slumped with disgust.

"I've never seen anything quite like that, have you? Those tiny little T-shirts over those great big—"

"Jack!"

"I'm sorry. You were saying?"

"It's only one-fifteen, but half the people in there are clearly dead drunk. And the food," she said, pointing to a menu posted in the window. "I've never seen so much cholesterol in one place in my life."

"There's a salad on it," he said.

"Where?"

He pointed. "Right there."

She leaned in close to read. "Fried chicken salad? With ranch dressing?"

"I'm sure there's some rabbit food in there. Come on. It's cold out here, and I'm starving. It'll be fine. Trust me."

Trust me. If he said that one more time...

Before she could protest further, he took her by the arm and hustled her inside. The hostess greeted them and showed them to a table by the window, which Rachel immediately objected to. They ended up at the back of the room beside the bar.

"Great table," he muttered.

"It's out of the way."

"It's practically in Cleveland."

She picked up her menu. "Good. We won't be spotted."

Jack frowned. "The only way we'd be spotted back here is if we sent up a flare."

A waitress swung by their table, a thirty-something woman who had plenty of the physique that appeared to be a job requirement, and Rachel noticed that she wasn't the least bit averse to showing it off to Jack. With her breasts less than a foot from his face, she recited a few specials, then gave him a suggestive little smile that said if he'd only dump the *boring* woman he was with, she could show him a really good time.

"What'll it be?" she asked.

"Rachel?" Jack said. "Have you decided?"

"Yes. Just bring me a side salad with vinaigrette dressing, and a glass of water."

The waitress rolled her eyes a little, made a note on her pad, then turned to Jack with a big smile. "How about you, honey?"

"Bring me a bacon cheeseburger with everything, and a side of curly fries." He pointed to the next table, where a pair of diners were sipping multicolored concoctions in tall, curvy glass. "What are those?"

"Colorado Comas."

"What's in them?"

"Everything but battery acid. And you get to keep the glass."

"Bring us a couple of those, too. And while you're at it, will you change her side salad to one of those fried chicken salads?"

"Gotcha." The waitress winked at him as she collected their menus, then sashayed off toward the kitchen.

"Jack!" Rachel said.

He turned to her with an innocent expression.

"What did you do that for?"

"You mean, why did I order some real food that you might actually enjoy?"

She huffed with disgust. "Fine. I'll just pick around the fried chicken chunks. And you just wasted all kinds of money, because I'm not touching one of those drinks."

"Then don't think for a minute that you're getting the glass."

She gave him a deadpan look. "Why don't you order six so you'll have a matched set?"

He raised his eyebrows. "That's not a bad idea."

She sighed with disgust. "This place is so tacky."

"Nah. It's just a little quirky."

"Yeah. Like our waitress. If she'd batted those fake eyelashes at you one more time, they'd have gone flying across the room."

He grinned. "Can I help it if I'm irresistible?"

Yes. He could help it. For once in his life, he could think about cutting her and every other woman in the vicinity a little slack. It was clear now that she was no more immune to him than that waitress was, and that was saying a lot. One minute she was going to order room service, and the next he'd maneuvered her into sitting in a loud, vulgar restaurant that actually had an appetizer of fried cheese and buffalo wings called "Heart Attack on a Plate." The only good thing about the place was that she couldn't think of a solitary soul she worked with who'd be caught dead here.

A few minutes later the waitress brought their drinks. Rachel stared at her glass with total disbelief.

"Try it," Jack said. "You might actually like it."

"No, thank you."

He pulled a ten-dollar bill from his wallet and slapped it onto the table. "I'll give you ten bucks to take one sip."

Rachel stared at him in disbelief. "Are you nuts?"

"So what if I am? It's easy money. Go for it."

With a nonchalant shrug, she took a sip. It tasted like a slushy blend of tropical fruit juices with a touch of alcohol. No big deal.

She took the bill and stuck it into her purse. He pulled out another ten and held it up.

"Care to go another round?"

There wasn't a shred of doubt left. He *was* nuts. "I don't know why I work for a living. This is so much easier."

"So take another drink."

She took another sip, a little longer one this time, since it always made her feel guilty if she didn't really earn her pay. She plucked the ten from between his fingers and stuck it into her purse alongside the other one. When she looked back, she was shocked to see him hauling out another one.

"Okay, okay!" she said. "I'll drink the stupid thing! Have you no sense at all about the value of a dollar? You just paid me twenty bucks to drink fruit juice."

He sat back in the booth. "Is that what it tastes like?"

She sipped it again. "Uh-huh. Pretty much."

Actually it was good. A whole bunch better than she thought it would be. She took another sip and felt the icy liquid slide down her throat. In fact, it was really, *really* good.

"And with all this fruit juice," she said, "it's probably got lots of vitamin C."

"So it's practically a health drink."

"Well, of course not." She took another sip. "Well, maybe. Sort of. With the fruit juice, and all."

And after a few more luscious sips, she discovered that she really didn't care much about vitamins one way or the other. A pleasant warmth melted through her, and all at once the music didn't seem so loud. No, it seemed loud, but somehow it kind of pulsed inside her head in a way that was...nice.

Soon the waitress brought them their order. She looked down at her salad, which was covered with fried chicken chunks. Very weird. She shoved the chicken into a little pile, segregating them from the lettuce. Healthy on one side, deadly on the other.

"It really was nice of Walter to bring all his employees on a retreat," Jack said. "Not many bosses would spend the money or take the time."

"Yeah. He's an okay guy, I guess," Rachel said, taking a bite of salad. She didn't realize until it was in her mouth that a small chicken chunk must have been hiding beneath that particular piece of romaine. Of course, she couldn't spit it out; that would be disgusting.

"You seem uptight around him," Jack said.

"That's because he's my boss."

"This is a vacation. You should be relaxing."

"I can't. A new project manager position is opening up. Walter's getting ready to make a decision about it, and I can't afford to slip up right now."

"What's the project?"

"A casino and luxury hotel in Reno."

"Now, there you go. Reno. A hell of a good place to build a hotel like that god-awful thing we're staying in."

"Hey, that resort is the pride and joy of my colleagues."

"And what about you?"

She opened her mouth, then closed it again. In spite of the whopper she'd told about having a husband, lying didn't come easily to her.

"That's what I thought," Jack said. "You think it's a monstrosity, too."

"I do not!"

"Uh-huh. If there's one thing I know about you—aside from the fact that you have a really ticklish spot just below your right ear—"

She rolled her eyes.

"—it's that a place like that offends your sensibilities just as much as it offends mine."

"Places like that," she said, "are what my firm does best. Actually it's what I do best, too."

"You mean it's what will get you promoted."

She raised her chin. "Yes. Exactly. Assuming you don't say or do something in the next few days that sends my career down the toilet."

"Hadn't planned on it. Who's your competition?"

"There's really only one person. Phil Wardman. But I'm more qualified than he is."

"Phil Wardman? That jerk we sat with at dinner last night?"

Rachel blinked. "Jerk?"

"Okay. Now I get it. I thought he was just a generalized ass-kisser. I didn't know he had a specific goal. Particularly the same goal you've got. Not that I have anything against ass-kissing. I just hate to see it done poorly."

Rachel looked at him with total amazement.

"There has to be something to base all the sucking up

on," Jack explained. "A germ of truth in all the platitudes, or some kind of connection with the suckee, or sooner or later it sounds phony. Wardman seems to be nothing but a yes-man."

Rachel was amazed. Jack had seen all that over one dinner?

"You really think he's just putting on?" she asked. "That he and Walter really aren't that buddy-buddy with each other?"

"Hard to say at this point. A guy like Walter warms up to anybody who looks like they're having a good time, and Wardman clearly knows how to play right into that."

"So you think all that sucking up means Phil has a better chance at the job than I do?"

"If the ability to kiss ass is the number one qualification, I'd say he's got you beat hands down."

Rachel slumped with disappointment.

"But it's not a problem. All you have to do is fight fire with fire."

"What do you mean?"

"Kiss a little ass yourself."

She sighed. "I can't. I'm lousy at that kind of thing."

"It's not hard. Get next to Walter, laugh at his jokes if they're remotely funny, let him know you're having a wonderful time on his orchestrated vacation, even if it's a stretch, and you're in. You don't have to be phony. Just interactive. He wants everybody to have a good time, and he's going to be hurt if you don't. Phil gives him what he wants. A great big smile."

"A smile?"

"Yeah. It beats the hell out of a frown. You know, that thing that was on your face through most of dinner last night."

"I was frowning?" Rachel felt a surge of anxiety. "I was hoping my face was more like...neutral."

"Nope. It was a frown. And why do that when it takes less effort to smile? Fewer muscles involved, so I've heard."

"I've heard that before, too, but I don't believe it. Smiling goes against gravity."

"So stand on your head if you have to, but put a smile on your face. Believe me, sweetheart, if you do that, not a man in sight will know that Wardman is even in the room."

Jack got the ball rolling with a broad, brilliant smile of his own that coaxed one right out of her. She just couldn't help it. Seeing those warm little crinkles around his mouth and that dimple in his left cheek made it impossible for her not to smile back.

"Now, see?" he said. "Is that so hard?"

"Not right now it isn't," she said. "But whenever I get around my boss, it feels phony."

"Do it anyway. It's called 'playing the game.' If all the sucking up in this country suddenly stopped, the American business community would fall apart at the seams."

This was exactly what Rachel had been afraid of. Some sort of ritual she had no idea how to participate in. That there was going to be more involved in getting that job than technical expertise. Like...socializing. She took another big sip of the goofy drink and wondered if it was something she'd ever feel comfortable with.

"If you'd only told me what the deal was before we went to dinner last night," Jack said, "we could have been on the offensive from the get-go."

"We? What do you mean, we?"

"I've noticed that you don't exactly enjoy leaping right into the middle of a conversation. I can help with that."

She held up her palm. "No, Jack. Please. Don't help me."

"Trust me. It'll be okay. We need to get the attention off Wardman and onto you."

"No! I don't want any attention on me!"

"Sure you do. You want that promotion, don't you?"

She closed her eyes.

"Take it easy, sweetheart. All you have to do is be yourself."

"I *am* being myself!"

"What? Suspicious, skeptical and paranoid?"

She glared at him. "Thanks, Jack. I appreciate that."

"Hey, all I meant was that if you just have a good time, everything else will follow. I mean, how hard is it to talk to people, anyway?"

Rachel sighed. "It's just not something that has ever come easily to me. As long as I'm talking about technical stuff, I'm fine. I can give a great presentation. But anything else..."

"You've never had any trouble talking to me."

"Oh, please. There's not a person on the planet who you couldn't get to talk. I swear you could charm a mannequin to life if you set your mind to it."

He grinned. "So you really think I'm charming?"

She rolled her eyes. "Well, I can see that *you* don't have any trouble taking compliments."

"I'm just enjoying the fact that it's coming from you."

She felt a little swirl of pleasure when he said that. She'd never been at ease when she dated, and first dates were such nightmares that she rarely went out with men she didn't already know pretty well. And flirting? Well that was completely out of the question. But that day in San Antonio, it had taken Jack about two minutes to wear down her usual defenses, and she'd felt more connected with him than with men she'd dated for months. She felt just as comfortable around him now, in spite of the fact that he was a ticking time bomb just waiting to explode. He *was* charming, and he could probably get anyone to believe just about anything—even the biggest lie she'd ever told in her life.

She poked around at her salad some more, spearing a lettuce leaf and the chicken chunk it was camouflaging. She put them both into her mouth and chewed with relish. Tacky restaurant. Great food. It had been a long time since she'd had anything that was deep fried, and it tasted wonderful.

"Good chicken, huh?" Jack said.

She stopped midchew, then gave up trying to hide it. "Okay, yes. It's good. And it's going straight to my hips as we speak."

He shoved his plate aside, then rested his forearms on the table and stared at her long and hard. "Life's too short to deprive yourself of things you really like. It's time you learned to live a little."

At this moment, she believed that. Wholeheartedly. She felt warm and a little woozy, and positively wonderful. The drink was good. The chicken was great. And Jack was...

Jack was just as she remembered. That warm smile, that beautiful body she'd wanted to keep on touching forever. She dropped her gaze to his lips, full, soft, sensuous lips that had felt like heaven against hers. Suddenly she had the most outrageous thought that if she had to go through the rest of her life without ever kissing him again, there was no point in living.

Some really wild song had started to play, and for some reason a lot of people were getting up from their tables, but Rachel barely noticed. She felt a warm buzzing sensation in her head, blocking out everything else, until it felt as if she and Jack were the only two people on the planet. The music seemed to grow louder, and people were moving somehow—dancing?—but all she could think about was the man she was with, who was staring back at her with that look on his face that said there wasn't anywhere else he'd rather be. The mere thought of that made her heart rate pick up considerably, an interesting contrast to the way everything else around her seemed to be moving in slow motion.

Then out of the blue a female hand snaked out and grabbed Jack by the wrist. Rachel looked up to see their waitress pulling him to his feet, and before she knew it, Jack had grabbed her hand and was pulling her right along with them.

"Jack! What the—"

"Conga line!"

Huh?

She was soon aware of the loud music with the heavy beat, and to her surprise, Jack drew her around and placed her in front of him in a long line of people.

"Jack! What are you—"

"Just go with it! Follow the person in front of you!"

She felt Jack's hands on her shoulders, and before it really dawned on her what she was doing, she'd put her hands on the man's shoulders in front of her. And then her feet were moving like all the others in a strange kind of left and right motion.

The conga. She'd seen it done at some goofy Caribbean resort on the Travel Channel, but she'd never expected to be doing it herself. Now she was. She was dancing along with the line as it made its way around the restaurant, the room spinning, the music pulsing through her. It was as if she was outside her body, looking at herself doing something really strange and not being able to do anything about it, but not even *wanting* to do anything about it, because all at once her heart was beating wildly and her mouth was smiling, and then she was actually *singing along* with the stupid song.

It felt *good*.

Then the music stopped, and the line came to a halt. Everyone in the place shouted and applauded, and she felt Jack's arm slip around her shoulders and pull her right up next to him. Startled, she glanced up to find him staring at her, and all at once she had a startling revelation.

He was going to kiss her.

Just as she was thinking that maybe she ought to do something to stop that from happening, a little devil appeared on her shoulder, the same one who'd convinced her to go crazy in San Antonio, and started whispering in her ear.

Look at his eyes. Can't you tell he wants you? He looks great. He feels great. You know for a fact that he is great, in bed and out. Six feet, two inches of pure, unadulterated pleasure. So why in the world do you want to push him away?

She didn't.

As the noisy crowd continued to applaud, Jack slid his hand along her neck, tilted her head up and lowered his mouth to hers.

Oh, yes.

For several long, heavenly moments they came together in a mating of hands and lips and tongues that was so incredible she wondered why she'd ever thought it was a bad idea. She'd been so shocked at her predicament when he kissed her in her office that she hadn't been able to truly enjoy the experience, but she was suffering from no such tension now.

Atta girl, the little devil said. Go for it.

She felt deliciously dizzy, maybe from the drinking, maybe from the dancing, but most assuredly from the fact that Jack was kissing her as if he couldn't get enough of her. Yes, the devil had essentially made her do it, but it was most definitely a collaborative effort. One she was enjoying to the fullest.

"Hey, you two! Didn't expect to see you here!"

Shocked at the familiar voice, Rachel spun around, and instantly she knew she was in deep, deep trouble.

Megan was standing right behind her.

9

RACHEL YANKED HERSELF AWAY from Jack, sending that nasty little devil tumbling off her shoulder and falling straight back to hell where he belonged.

"Sorry," Megan said. "Didn't mean to interrupt."

It took Rachel a moment to get her bearings, to realize what she'd done, and that it really was *Megan* who'd seen it. Megan, with her eagle eyes and her total weirdness and her gossipy mouth that was soon to be moving at the speed of light. Before the day was out, she'd be telling the entire world that she'd seen Rachel in this tacky place, dancing like a fool and putting on a public display of affection that would put a cheap hooker to shame.

So much for nobody she knew being caught dead in this place.

"You didn't interrupt a thing," she said.

"Sure she did," Jack said. "The best kiss I've had all day."

He winked at Megan, and Rachel wanted to send him south right along with the devil.

"Wow, Rachel," Megan said. "You've never struck me as the conga type."

"I'm not. Not really. Sometimes Jack...insists."

Megan grinned. "Good job, Jack. I can't even get her to take her suit coat off at the office."

"Why don't we sit down?" Jack said, putting his arm around Rachel's shoulders and shuffling her toward their table. Good thing, because she was suddenly feeling a little faint. He pulled out her chair and she plopped down. There, that felt better. Now she saw only two of everything instead of four. And looking down at the remnants of her drink pooling at the bottom of her glass, she realized just how badly her taste buds had been fooled. There must have been enough alcohol in that fruit juice to set an iceberg on fire.

Then Jack grabbed a chair from an adjoining table and pulled it up to theirs, inviting Megan to join them. Was he crazy? Did he not know that this woman's dream job was to be a reporter for the *National Enquirer*?

"What are you doing here?" she asked Megan.

"The resort is a little stuffy, so I asked the concierge to recommend someplace a little off-the-wall that might actually be fun. He sent me here."

Rachel turned to look at Jack, and he looked back at her innocently. It was all she could do not to kick him under the table.

Megan caught the waitress's eye and pointed to the glasses on their table, asking for one of whatever they were having. Good, Rachel thought. If Megan drank one of those, she might develop alcohol-induced amnesia and forget she'd even been here at all.

A few minutes later, the waitress set the drink down in front of Megan. She took a long sip on the straw, then smiled. "Ah, my kind of beverage. The kind that sneaks up on you, then smacks you one."

Well, that was one way of putting it.

"Having fun at the retreat so far?" Jack asked Megan.

Megan shrugged. "It's okay. Like I said, a little stuffy. But it's good to get away from Denver for a while."

"Have you been skiing yet?"

"Nah. I don't ski. I'd rather sit in front of the fire with a drink in my hand." She took another sip of her drink, then nodded down at Jack's hand. "Interesting."

"What?" Jack said.

"Rachel wears a wedding ring. You don't. Why is that?"

Rachel stared dumbly at Jack's left hand right along with Megan, feeling a sudden rush of anxiety.

Her husband wasn't wearing a wedding ring.

It was the most obvious thing of all. The *most* obvious. How could she have forgotten to address that little detail?

She opened her mouth, but nothing came out. She had no idea what to say. None at all. She glanced at Jack. *Please,* she pleaded silently. *If you've ever shot from the hip and hit the target, do it now.*

"Well," Jack said, looking not the least bit flustered, "I was wearing one, right up to a few days ago. Then I had something come up when I was leaving Bogotá." He slid his hand over Rachel's and gave her a smile. "And I'm married to the most wonderful woman in the world for understanding."

She smiled back at him. *Yes. Of course I understand. Just tell me what it is I'm so understanding about.*

"Before I left for the airport, I was mugged."

Huh?

"By a teenage boy. He had a knife. He couldn't have been more than thirteen years old. He told me to give him my jewelry, my watch, my cash. I relieved him of the knife and told him to get lost."

"Really?" Megan said. "So what happened?"

"I started to walk away. Then I looked back. He was sitting on the curb. Crying."

"Crying?" Megan said.

"Yes. There had just been a three-day rainstorm, and he told me his family's home had been flooded. They lost everything. He was the oldest of five children, no father. He was just trying to find a way to help his family."

Megan's eyes were growing bigger by the moment. "So what happened then?"

"I gave him everything I had on me. My watch, my cash...and my ring."

"You're kidding."

"No. I knew Rachel would understand."

Rachel froze, her hand still inside Jack's. As she watched Megan's face, there was nothing but skepticism. Definite skepticism. She knew it was a lie. Every word. She knew it was a lie, and now—

"I'll bet he was faking you out," Megan said. "Gave you a sob story, then cleaned you out."

Rachel breathed a sigh of relief. Yes, Megan knew someone was lying, and Rachel was just glad she thought it was Jack's mythical penniless child.

Jack shrugged. "Maybe he was." He paused. "But what if he wasn't?"

Megan took another sip of her drink. "Trust me. You gave up your wedding ring to a kid who was playing you like a drum." She turned to Rachel. "What did you think when your husband came home without his ring?"

"I thought...I thought how lucky I was to be married to such a wonderful man."

She forced a smile in Jack's direction. Megan stared at Jack's hand for another moment or two, then settled back in her chair and took another sip of her drink.

Rachel tried to relax. Megan had bought it. She'd actually bought it. But why not? Nobody on earth sounded more sincere than Jack, even when he was being insincere. Still, there was something about one lie being heaped on top of another one that made Rachel sick to her stomach.

Or maybe it was the drink. Or the fried chicken chunks. Or the conga dancing.

Or all of the above.

Whatever it was, it was making her extremely nauseated.

She shoved her chair back and stood up. "Excuse me. I...I have to go to the ladies' room."

The last thing she wanted to do was leave Jack alone with Megan, but she had no choice, not with the way her stomach was churning right now. She just had to trust that he'd hold his own until she could get herself together again. Then she'd come back out, grab him, get back to the hotel, duck into their room and be very, very careful about ever coming out again.

JACK WATCHED RACHEL WEAVE her way toward the ladies' room, wishing he'd pondered the issue of being minus a wedding ring before somebody thought to ask him about it. It was the kind of detail that he really should have been prepared for, but then again, there wasn't anything he couldn't explain with a little quick thinking. All in all, he'd been able to cover pretty well. Megan seemed to believe it, anyway. No problem. He'd pulled it off.

"Bet it's hot down there in Columbia this time of year," Megan said.

"Yeah. That's why it's nice to come to a place where it's snowing."

"Do you spend a lot of time in the sun down there?"

"More than I care to."

Megan nodded. "So," she said, swirling her straw around in her drink. "Why are you and Rachel pretending to be married when you're really not?"

Jack froze, his heart suddenly beating double-time. For a moment he was speechless, which was a very unfamiliar state, but he hadn't counted on this. He'd allowed for a little suspicion from Rachel's co-workers, but this was out-and-out accusation. Had the story he'd just told tripped him up somehow?

"Uh...what do you mean?"

"You two aren't really married, are you?"

"Not married?" he said. "Of course we are. What makes you think we're not?"

She nodded toward his hand. "The tan line. Or lack of one."

"What?"

"You've supposedly been in South America. Bogotá is close to the equator. If you'd had a ring on for even a few days down there, you'd have a tan line around your finger. You've got no tan line. Chances are you've never even worn a ring on that finger, much less given it to some poor kid and his destitute family."

Jack glanced down at his left hand. She was right. *Damn.* He hadn't counted on somebody like Megan, who sucked up all the details of her surroundings and processed them with the speed of a microchip.

"I'm right, aren't I?" she said.

He sighed with resignation. "Good catch."

"Thank you. I pride myself on my powers of observation. So are you really a doctor?"

"Afraid not. I own a construction company."

She shifted around to face him. "Okay. There's a story here, and I want to hear it. Why in the world are the two of you pretending to be married?"

There was nothing else Jack could do now but spill his guts and throw himself on the mercy of his accuser. Anything less, and she'd catch him in yet another lie.

He glanced toward the bathroom door, wondering how soon Rachel might be coming out. Judging from how green her face looked when she got up from the table, it could be a while.

He told Megan the whole story. Everything. Including why Rachel had made up a husband in the first place.

"Yeah," Megan said, "Walter has a real thing about married employees. The only reason I squeaked in is because I worked there as a temporary first. I did a good job, so he hired me, lack of husband and all."

Then Jack explained the origin of the photograph on Rachel's credenza, and how he'd come to be the one she was passing off as her husband.

Megan's eyes flew open wide. "You mean to tell me that when I dragged you back to her office, you hadn't seen each other in six months?"

"Right."

"And then only for one night?"

"Right."

She grinned. "This is really wild."

He put a hand against her arm. "You've got to promise me you won't tell anyone."

"Me? The office gossip? Not tell anyone?" She let out a long breath. "Wow. I don't know. If I try to hold on to something this good, I could explode."

"And if this gets out, it could hurt Rachel. I don't want that to happen. Will you keep our secret?"

She twisted her mouth with disgust.

"Please?"

"Oh, stop looking at me like that, will you? I'm a sucker for a good-looking man, particularly a good-looking man who knows how to beg." She sighed dramatically. "I won't tell anyone. I promise. And my word is pretty solid, too, believe it or not."

Jack smiled. "I believe it."

"You know, Rachel is way more devious than I thought. I like that in a person."

"The job was important to her. And she seems to be very competent at what she does. Am I right?"

"The truth? She's the best. I'm just not sure why she has to be so stuffy."

"Because she's trying to be the best."

"You can have fun on the way to the top. It's not a crime."

"I know that. You know that. Rachel—she doesn't know that. But there is a little more going on under her surface than you realize."

"Oh, yeah?"

"Picture a mountain in the Alps. Dead of winter. Snow all over the place."

"Yeah?"

"Now imagine that underneath all that snow, that mountain is really a volcano."

Megan's eyes widened. "Really?"

"Really."

"Hmm. Maybe you're right. I saw you lay that kiss on her a minute ago, and she didn't seem to mind that."

"Exactly. And I'd like to lay a few more on her before this vacation is over."

"So you actually blackmailed her into letting you come along on this trip?"

"Now, let's not use the word *blackmail*. It was more like I saw an opportunity and went for it."

Megan eyed him carefully. "You know, I've seen the way you look at her, and it's not phony. You really are crazy about her, aren't you?"

Jack's smile faded. "All I know is that when I saw her on that street in Denver, I wasn't going to stop until I found her again."

Megan sighed. "She doesn't realize how lucky she is."

"Right now, I'm having a hard time convincing her of that."

"She's smart. She's devious. Too bad she's also blind."

"I've got three days left to open her eyes."

Megan smiled. "Good luck."

"Oh, quick question. Tell me about Phil Wardman."

"He's a twit."

"Any real competition for Rachel for the project manager position?"

"Hard to say. She deserves it. But I'm telling you, if she doesn't open her mouth once in a while and *speak*, he's going to grab it right out from under her."

Jack nodded. "Thanks for the info."

"Anytime." Megan rose from her chair. "Maybe I'd better go collect Rachel from the bathroom floor."

"I'd appreciate that. And, Megan?"

"Yeah?"

"I don't think Rachel would like it too much if the world found out that she was full of alcohol up to her eyeballs and dancing in a conga line."

Megan sighed. "You're not leaving me with much here, are you?"

"Thanks for keeping this just between us."

She smiled. "No problem. I actually like her, you know. Even if she is a little uptight."

"I'm going to loosen her up. Mark my words."

"And I think you're just the man for the job. If you need any help, though, let me know. The only thing I like better than gossiping is matchmaking."

"Stay on your toes. I just might take you up on that."

"I'M NEVER GOING TO FORGIVE you for this, Jack. Never. Not if I live to be a hundred."

Rachel lay on the bed in their sexually overblown hotel room, her head pounding like crazy, thinking what a fool she'd been to let Jack talk her into going to that horrible restaurant. He sat on the end of the bed, smiling as if this was funny. There was nothing funny about it.

"I guess there was a little more alcohol in those drinks than we thought, huh?" he said.

"A little more? A *little?*"

"The glasses are nice," he said, nodding toward the bar, where he'd placed those weird glasses he'd insisted on bringing back with them.

"No. They're not nice. They're stupid."

"Does this mean I can have both of them?"

Rachel rolled her eyes, even though it hurt to do it. "I can't believe I got sick. I've never done that before."

"I think you'd have been okay if not for the conga. It kind of shook things up."

"Didn't I tell you I didn't want any part of that place?"

"Come on, Rachel. Didn't you have a good time? Just a little?"

"Oh, yeah. I had a ball. Eating food that clogged my arteries, dancing like an idiot, getting spotted by the office gossip and getting sick in the ladies' room. You really know how to show a girl a good time."

He smiled. "You forgot about the kiss."

Rachel closed her eyes. "No, I haven't forgotten. But I intend to. Megan, on the other hand, will never forget. She's probably telling everybody within earshot what she saw."

"No, she's not."

"How do you know that?"

"Because I asked her not to."

"Oh, like that's going to stop her?"

"It will."

"You don't know Megan."

"You don't know my powers of persuasion."

Rachel would have to take issue with that. She knew very well his powers of persuasion.

"No. She's going to tell everyone, and then it'll get back to Walter what a weird person I am. I try my best to look professional around my boss, and now she's going to tell him—"

"Hey, even if she did say something, so what? There's nothing wrong with having a good time. As I told you, that's what Walter wants."

"Yes. Within the bounds of good taste. I stepped way outside that this afternoon, and it's all your fault."

"My fault?"

"You bribed me to drink."

"Can I help it you like easy money?"

"And dragged me along to dance—"

"You could have stopped anytime you wanted to."

"And then you kissed me. Right out there in front of everybody."

He raised an eyebrow. "I didn't see you putting up much of a fight at the time."

He was right, of course, and that embarrassed her even more. She'd wanted him to kiss her. At that moment, she'd wanted it desperately. So why did she feel like such a fool now?

Because she'd been taught from the time she was a child that appearances were everything. Her mother's single raised eyebrow was all it had ever taken to make Rachel tug her skirt closer to her knees, sit up straighter or pull her elbows off the table. After all, little indiscretions could turn into big ones, and the last thing she wanted was to follow in her sister's footsteps.

Laura, five years her senior, had thought nothing of

stealing gin from the liquor cabinet, staying out all night, or inviting her boyfriend of the moment to her bedroom on the sly for a little after-hours sex. Currently on her third marriage, she'd practically made a career of falling for crazy, unstable men and systematically ruining her life.

Their parents had lost the battle with Laura. They'd had no intention of losing it with Rachel.

Even now, when she thought about the stone-cold looks of disapproval that came over her parents' faces whenever they talked about her sister, it made Rachel shudder. But they were right. Her sister had succumbed to things that felt good at the moment, and that lack of self-discipline and inability to stay on the right path had eventually screwed up her life. Rachel had no intention of screwing up hers.

What alarmed her the most right now was her own lack of self-control where Jack was concerned. Today she'd gotten off light. It had only been a kiss. But if she let him have his way, the next thing she knew, he'd be living out that fantasy he'd described by dragging her into the nearest public bathroom stall and having his way with her.

"Never mind the kiss," she told Jack. "The worst part was that story you told Megan about why you weren't wearing a wedding ring. You went way over the top with that one."

His smile faded. "Oh? Why do you say that?"

"Okay, maybe she bought it because you're supposedly Dr. Jack Kellerman, medical humanitarian. A real benevolent kind of guy. Still, you told her you gave your wedding band to a kid for his homeless family? Please. Couldn't you have come up with something a little more believable than that?"

For maybe the first time since he'd shown up at her office the day before yesterday, Jack's teasing manner died away and his expression grew serious.

"For your information, Rachel, the story is true."

"True? Oh, please. Dr. Jack Kellerman is a figment of my imagination. And you've certainly never been on the streets of Bogotá."

"No, but I have been on the streets of San Antonio. Every year I spend two weeks doing volunteer work. I help build houses so low-income people can own their own homes."

Rachel stared at him with disbelief. Volunteer work? For two weeks at a time?

"When I was leaving a work site late one night," he went on, "a kid tried to mug me. No, I didn't have a wedding ring to give him, but by the time we sat down on the curb and had a long talk and he wiped the tears off his face, my wallet was empty and I was minus a watch."

"You're kidding. You actually did that?"

His eyes narrowed. "Do you think I'm lying about it?"

"Well, no—"

"Then why do you find it so surprising?"

"I—I don't know. I guess because you just don't seem like..."

"Like what? The kind of guy who can get serious long enough to do something worthwhile?"

"I didn't say that."

"We may be talking about different people and different places," Jack said, "but I have invested time and money in other people who needed it desperately. So maybe the man you made up isn't as different from me as you seem to think."

"I just—I just didn't know all that about you. That's all."

He stood up. "There's a lot you don't know. Maybe you

should quit spending all your time trying to shove me away and use that effort to find out about the real me. You just might like what you see."

He turned and headed for the door.

"Where are you going?"

"Don't worry," he said, grabbing his coat. "I'll be back in time for the party tonight. Are we dressing up, or is it casual?"

"Casual."

"Then I'll see you there."

With that, he left the room, closing the door behind him.

Rachel stared after him, shocked by the sudden silence. She just sat there, wondering how the tables had turned so drastically.

This was bad.

Jack had left here alone, and now he was going to be running all over this resort, talking to God knew who, and before the day was out, her career could be...

No. That wasn't what she was worried about right now at all.

She flopped back against the pillow and stared at the ceiling. What worried her was the look on Jack's face as he left the room. Seeing that uncharacteristic mix of hurt and anger made her feel even sicker than she already did, because she was beginning to face facts. Jack Kellerman had a lot more going for him than a handsome face, a great body and an electric personality, and suddenly she was seeing him differently than she ever had before. She wanted to get to know him better.

A lot better.

And he was right. In spite of everything, she'd had fun today. Because of him.

She sighed, her head pounding. All she'd wanted during this retreat was to stay in control of the situation, but now she wasn't in control of anything. She'd thought her only problem was to make sure Jack didn't say or do anything to hurt her career. Now she had a second problem.

She'd fallen for him in a matter of hours in San Antonio, and it was happening all over again.

A SHOPPING MALL. What a hell of a thing to stick in the middle of the Rocky Mountains.

Jack killed most of the afternoon walking around the resort, taking in the splashy sights. His tour culminated with a visit to the mall, a structure that he discovered was even more ostentatious on the inside than it was on the outside.

After strolling past a carbon copy of every trendy franchise in America, Jack stopped at the food court, bought a cup of overpriced coffee, then sat down at a table and stared at the passersby, wondering what in the hell he was doing at this resort in the first place.

In spite of the time he and Rachel had shared together in San Antonio, the moment he found out just how uptight she could be, he should have run the other way and never looked back. And now that he knew how she saw him—somebody who was fun every once in a while, but had the depth of a mud puddle—he really had no reason to hang around at all.

He was surprised at how much her comments had hurt. He'd always had a hide as tough as a rhinoceros, letting any insults life threw him roll right off his back. Not once had he ever felt the need to convince anyone that there might be more to him than met the eye, but somehow, with Rachel, it was important to him that she see beyond his laid-back exterior to the man beneath.

The man beneath. Now, there was a concept he'd never

spent much time thinking about. Rachel clearly hadn't, either. But after what had happened today, for some reason he was beginning to wish she would.

After a while, Jack tossed the remainder of his coffee into a trash can and continued through the mall, feeling more depressed with every step he took. This wasn't like him. Up to now, if a relationship didn't work out, no big deal. Smile and say goodbye. Move on down the road. So why was this different?

Maybe because he knew for a fact that something deep inside Rachel was screaming to get out, and he wanted to be around when it finally did. He'd felt so much in common with her six months ago that he simply refused to believe it had been an aberration. The face she showed to the world—that was the phony one, no matter how much she protested to the contrary.

He arrived at the center atrium of the mall, and what he saw stopped him dead in his tracks.

Towering two stories to the roof of the atrium was a mural—a big, colorful, stylistic mural filled with images of miners and mules and rivers and boomtowns and sweeping mountain vistas, depicting the raw, hectic life of Colorado's silver rush days. It curved along several angled walls, which were designed to allow traffic to flow through and around them. The exhibit was incorporated into the very structure of the building itself, using the natural light coming through the atrium windows to illuminate it. Glancing around, he saw carefully placed spotlights that probably provided a completely different view of the mural at night.

For the longest time he just stood there, letting people walk around him, as he stared up at the work of art, amazed at how the feeling of days gone by suddenly seemed fresh and alive. Right here in this spot, a little bit of Colorado history came to life, and he was in awe of the person who could pull off such a delicate balance between the old and the new.

Then he felt a jolt of sudden understanding. *I worked mainly on the shopping mall. The atrium area in particular.* Rachel.

All at once every snide remark he'd made about this place came back to him in a flood of condemnation. He knew now which talented person had melded art and architecture into a visual feast for the eyes. Because of her, even the most contemporary-minded person looking for glitz and glamour would be treated to a glimpse of Colorado history and fall in love with it.

Rachel didn't know all there was to know about him, that was for sure. But this atrium convinced him that maybe the reverse was also true. Plenty about her was left to be discovered, and he redoubled his resolve to do just that.

"So, RACHEL," MEGAN SAID, "Where's Jack? He is coming tonight, isn't he?"

Rachel stood with her co-worker along one wall of the Aspen Room, the wood-paneled, chandelier-lit room where tonight's get-together was being held. A huge stone fireplace burned logs of fragrant pine, and sofas and chairs were placed in comfortable groupings throughout the room. The party was already kicking off, with a band warming up, people milling around and waiters circling the floor.

She'd changed into a pair of black pants, a royal-blue turtleneck sweater, and a pair of high-heeled black boots. The entire time she was getting ready, she thought about Jack, and the more she thought about Jack, the more nervous she became. "Yes," she told Megan. "He'll be here. He's just running a little late."

Rachel checked her watch. Seven minutes late, to be exact. He'd promised to be here. Surely he hadn't changed his mind. She needed him here. After all, if he didn't come, it would be terribly awkward to try to explain his absence.

Stop lying to yourself. You want him here because of him.

She knew that a relationship with Jack, who was as different from her as night was from day, was the craziest idea on earth. But as evening drew nearer, a feeling of unrest overtook her—a nervous, jittery, breathless feeling that she'd experienced only once before. Six months ago in San Antonio. And now that she saw another side to Jack, it only made him that much more attractive.

Then she thought about how she'd insulted him, making assumptions about who he was because she'd never bothered to find out any more about him than what she saw on the surface. And that made her even more nervous about facing him again.

"Why, there he is," Megan said.

Rachel turned to see Jack standing at the doorway, dressed as he had been earlier in jeans, boots and a V-necked sweater over a T-shirt, looking so handsome that just a single glance at him made her melt inside.

Then his gaze locked on to hers.

For the span of at least ten seconds, neither one of them moved. She looked at his face for some kind of indication that he might still be angry, but she couldn't tell. All she knew was that if he didn't stop looking at her so intently, he was going to bore a hole right through her.

"So what's he just standing there for?" Megan asked. "Get him over here. It's time to get this party moving."

Rachel made her way across the room, circling the furniture, sidestepping a waiter, until she stood in front of him. And she still wasn't quite sure what to say.

"I was afraid you weren't going to come," she said softly.

"I told you I would."

"I know, but—"

"But you thought maybe I'd stay away anyway?"

"I—I wasn't sure."

"It might be easier for you if I did stay away. Then you wouldn't have to spend every second worrying about what I'm going to say."

"I'm not worried about what you're going to say. I just...I saw you across the room, and all I could think was..."

"That it would be a pretty awkward party if your husband didn't show up?"

"No. That it would be a pretty dull party if my husband didn't show up."

She hadn't planned on saying that, but she was beginning to think there had to be a lot of truth in words that slipped so easily from her lips. He looked surprised for a moment, then cracked a tiny smile.

"Gosh, Rachel. You're beginning to sound as if you want a little excitement in your life."

"Maybe I do." She smiled back at him, astonished at how good it felt. "I'm sorry for what I said earlier, Jack. I think it's wonderful that you use your talent and your time to help other people. I really am impressed. It seems there's more to you than meets the eye."

"Actually, I was a little impressed myself today."

"Really?"

"I took a walk around the mall."

She grinned. "You could bring yourself to do that?"

"It was much easier than I'd anticipated." He paused. "Particularly when I saw the atrium."

"Oh?" Her eyes widened a little. "And what did you think of it?"

"I thought," he said, "that there's more to Rachel Westover than meets the eye, too. You were responsible for that mural, weren't you? And the design that went along with it?"

She shrugged. "I may have had a little bit to do with it."

"A little bit?"

"Okay. Everybody was skeptical, but in the end the client loved it."

"Well, then. It seems I said a few things I shouldn't have, as well. And had a few misconceptions of my own."

Rachel felt a rush of elation, a sense that they were starting over from a place where they both had a more solid, respectful view of each other, and it felt wonderful.

"Megan was wondering where you were," Rachel said. "Apparently she doesn't think the party can start until you show up."

"Then I'd say it's our duty to get in there and make sure everybody has a good time." He dipped his head and brushed his lips against her cheek. "I promise you, Rachel—this is not going to be a dull night."

10

AS IT TURNED OUT, JACK was absolutely right.

Within a few minutes of his arrival, they sat down together on an overstuffed love seat, and soon the sofa and chairs in the vicinity were occupied and the conversation was flowing.

The group was a fluid one. One person would get up and another one would sit down, changing the direction of the conversation. But Rachel had no inclination to move somewhere else, and neither, it seemed, did Jack. They remained glued to the tiny love seat, chatting with anyone who happened by. The warmth of his body next to hers was intoxicating, and the way he draped his arm along the low back of the love seat behind her made her feel as if she were wrapped in a protective cocoon. Every once in a while, he would turn and give her one of those looks reserved for couples only, couples in love, couples who are merely tolerating the people around them because they have eyes only for each other. And as the evening progressed, that was exactly what it felt like.

In spite of her going three rounds with the Colorado Coma at lunch, Rachel eventually ordered a glass of wine and sipped it slowly, letting its warmth flow through her. Occasionally Jack would drop his hand to the back of her neck, and take the area beneath the collar of her sweater with his fingertips. It was a subtle act, but the effect on her was devastating. At the same time, he laughed, he listened, he told jokes—clean ones when the audience demanded it, and bawdy ones when it didn't. His good looks were a big part of his charm, at least where the women were concerned, but when it came right down to it, it was his personality that people seemed to gravitate toward.

But the best part was that instead of feeling uptight as she usually did in a crowd of people, Rachel actually felt relaxed. As the night progressed, something that had been nearly impossible for her all her life began to feel effortless. She knew if there were any of those awful pauses in conversation, Jack would intercede and take up the slack. She was free to contribute without having to shoulder the entire burden, and she found herself wondering what she'd ever done without him. She was starting to think that a lot, in more ways than one.

Then Walter and Emma sat down with them, and Rachel felt uneasy all over again. A few minutes later, Phil began to hover on the periphery, waiting for somebody to get up. As soon as a seat was free, he slid into the unoccupied chair and proceeded to try to monopolize the conversation. He might have succeeded, too, if not for Jack.

Jack caught Walter's eye. "I saw the mall atrium for the first time today."

Walter grinned. "It's really something, isn't it?"

"That's an understatement."

"I have to admit that I wasn't too sure about it in the beginning, but Rachel insisted on presenting the idea to the client. She sold everybody on it."

"It's no wonder. That's her passion, you know."

"What's that?"

"Nineteenth-century history. She's an expert."

"Oh?"

"You bet. Ask her anything. From Jesse James to the

Civil War to the California gold rush. She can tell you all about them."

Walter turned to Rachel. "You know, I'm a bit of a Civil War buff myself. Emma and I even went to a reenactment a few years ago. It was very exciting."

"Actually," Emma said, "Walter went to the reenactment. I went shopping."

Everybody laughed, but Walter's attention was focused squarely on Rachel. "I saw a program on cable the other day about the Reconstruction era. Fascinating stuff."

"I saw it, too," Rachel said. "It's one of a series of programs about the Civil War. The generals, the Underground Railroad, Lincoln's presidency—"

"Yes!" Walter said. "I've seen a few of those. But I missed the one on the battle of Gettysburg."

"I have it taped. If you'd like, I could bring it to the office for you."

Walter beamed. "That'd be great! I'd appreciate that."

Emma shook her head sadly. "Here we go again. Pretty soon he's going to want to put on one of those uniforms and actually take part in a reenactment."

"Hey, I just might do that," Walter said before turning back to Rachel. "Do you think they'd have room for a fifty-eight-year-old infantry soldier?"

"Why not? Plenty of real Civil War soldiers were older than that."

Emma rolled her eyes. "For heaven's sake, Rachel, don't encourage him. After all, there's only so much shopping I can do in one place."

Rachel laughed, and before she knew it, she'd launched into a discussion with Walter about post–Civil War politics, just the two of them, while conversation flowed in other directions all around them. With all the noise, she had to lean away from Jack to hear Walter as he spoke, but

Jack would frequently touch her thigh, or tease his hand against her shoulder—just something to remind her that he was still there, and he was still thinking about her. She became vaguely aware that Phil seemed a little miffed that she was monopolizing the big boss's time, but then she heard Jack ask him what he thought the Broncos' chances were this year for a playoff spot. Phil puffed up and started to orate on the subject of football from a former player's point of view, and soon he'd forgotten all about Walter. Rachel smiled to herself.

Thank you, Jack.

"Well," Walter said finally, "I could sit here and chat all night, but I'd better make the rounds. It's been fun talking to you, Rachel. Maybe when we get back to Denver, we can go to lunch and take up the discussion again."

"I'd like that," she replied.

Walter and Emma walked away, and Rachel leaned toward Jack, exhilarated by the fact that she'd actually carried on an extended conversation with her boss about something other than work, and he'd actually seemed to enjoy it.

"I've got to get up," she whispered to Jack.

"Don't go now," he said with a smile. "We were just getting comfortable."

"The ladies' room. Save my seat?"

"It's all yours, sweetheart."

As she stood up, he gave her a warm smile that said, *I'll be counting the minutes until you get back.* How much of that was for show and how much wasn't, she didn't know, but when she gave him a smile in return that said, *So will I,* she meant every bit of it.

She left the Aspen Room and went down a short hallway to the ladies' room. After washing her hands, she looked at herself in the mirror, and all at once she was strikingly aware of her own face, of the little lines around her mouth that were slightly turned down and the ones between her brows that were caused by them being drawn together with tension.

Frown lines.

Jack was right. She spent most of her time frowning. But not tonight. Tonight she was well on her way to teaching her face a whole new set of habits, and it was all because of Jack. But it wasn't just because of the conversation he'd so artfully begun for her. Every time he touched her, she felt as if she were an ice cube melting in his hands, and she couldn't wait to get back so he could liquefy her a little more.

She closed her eyes, acutely aware of the flutter in her stomach, the one that had started about the time Jack showed up tonight and showed no signs of going away, a feeling that scared her and exhilarated her at the same time. It was almost as if her brain was pulling her one way and her heart was pulling her another, but for tonight, she decided to go with her heart.

She combed her fingers through her hair, dabbed on a little lipstick, then came out of the bathroom and started back down the hall.

"Rachel."

She wheeled around, shocked to see Jack standing just behind a half-open door across the hall. What in the world was he doing?

"Come here," he whispered, motioning to her with his fingers.

Looking left and right and seeing no one in the vicinity, she walked warily to where he stood. He swung the door wide, took her by the arm and pulled her inside.

A quick glance told her they were in a large walk-in closet with floor-to-ceiling shelves, filled with sheets and towels. Jack closed the door. She heard a click, and suddenly they were plunged into darkness except for the band of light peeking beneath the door.

"Jack! What are you doing?"

To her surprise, he pulled her right up next to him, wrapping his arms around her.

"You had Walter eating out of your hand out there," he murmured. "A few more rounds of North and South trivia, and you'll be bonded forever. Everybody thinks you're positively charming. How does it feel?"

She placed her palms against his chest. "Jack, what are you up to?"

"No," he said, his voice becoming an intense whisper. "Think about it. How does it make you feel?"

How did it feel to finally have the attention of the big boss? To feel like part of the crowd? To feel, for once in her life, as if she wasn't on the outside looking in?

It felt *wonderful.*

"It's you they're really crazy about," she said. "Not me."

He swept her hair away from her cheeks, then cupped her face, stroking it with his thumbs. "No, it's you. I've been watching you all night. You've never looked more beautiful."

Her heart fluttered wildly. "Remember what I said... about touching..."

"I've been touching you all night."

"But not while we're...alone. You know what I meant."

"No, I'm afraid I don't. Next time you'd better say exactly what you mean, or I'm liable to get a little confused. And when I get confused, there's no telling what I might do."

"But somebody...somebody might see us..."

"The door's closed."

"Hear us, then."

"Are you planning on doing some screaming?"

"Of course not!"

"Give me a few minutes," he said, "and I might change your mind about that."

Speculation about just how he intended to do that made her heart lurch wildly. To her surprise, though, he moved away, his back to the door.

"Jack? What are you doing?"

She felt nothing. Heard nothing. Then his voice came out of the darkness, hot and sex-laced.

"Take off your sweater."

Rachel gulped. "What?"

"Right now. The bra, too. I want to touch you."

"Jack, don't to this to me. Let me out of this closet."

"You can walk out of here anytime you want to. I won't stop you." He paused. "But if you stay here, you have to do as I say."

For several seconds she stood motionless, swearing she could hear him breathe. Her eyes were adjusting to the darkness, but she could just barely make out his silhouette. She knew this was insane. She knew she should walk out of here. But for some reason she couldn't fathom, she felt rooted to the spot where she stood.

"You're still here," he said.

But why? They were in a linen closet, and he wanted her naked. She should be walking out. *Running* out.

Yet she wasn't.

"I can't see you clearly right now," he murmured, "but I know your cheeks are bright red. Am I right?"

"I—I don't know."

"Oh, you know. You can't help but know. Touch them. They're on fire."

She put her hands to her cheeks and couldn't believe how hot they felt.

"They get that way every time you're embarrassed, don't they?"

She paused, her hands still against her cheeks. "Yes."

"Did you know they flush when you're excited, too?"

She yanked her hands away.

"Which is it, Rachel? Are you embarrassed or excited?"

She felt as if she couldn't even catch her breath. *Both.*

"The sweater," he said. "Off."

"I can't! Somebody might—"

Click.

"What was that?"

"I locked the door. Nobody's coming in."

"If they have a key—"

"Take off your sweater."

She'd never felt anything so illicit in her entire life. This was crazy. Insane. She felt as if she were caught inside some kind of sexual vortex where even the most outrageous acts were acceptable as long as they happened under the cover of darkness.

Just like last night.

She took a deep breath, then pulled her sweater off over her head, unable to believe that she was actually doing it, but wanting to do it.

"Drop it," Jack said.

She did.

"Now the bra."

She paused only a moment before unhooking the front clasp of her bra, then easing the straps off her shoulders. The air was cold, making her nipples contract instantly. She dropped the bra, its tiny hook clicking against the tile floor.

"Don't move," he said.

"Jack—"

"Not one muscle."

She heard the soft scuff of his boots as he stepped toward her, then felt his hands close around her wrists. He pushed her gently against the wall. She jumped at his shadowed touch, and he waited, not moving, until she stilled. He held her arms at her sides and moved closer until she felt his hot breath only a scant inch from her ear. A warm, masculine smell filled her nostrils, mingling with the scent of his sweater. With every second that passed, she slipped further and further from reality, right back into that fantasy world Jack knew precisely how to create.

"I know what you like," he whispered.

He did. Better than any man alive. And it sounded as if he was getting ready to prove it.

"You like it when I kiss you here." He touched his lips to her neck just below her right ear, sending hot shivers down her spine.

"And here."

He kissed the curve of her jaw.

"And here."

He smoothed his lips along the column of her neck, and almost involuntarily, she tilted her head back, allowing him better access. He closed his lips over the curve between her neck and shoulder and sucked gently, just enough that she knew it would leave a mark.

She wanted to touch him, was desperate to, but still he held her arms at her sides. Just his lips. They were the only other things she felt. And she didn't know where they were going next.

He kissed her collarbone, then moved lower to tease his lips against the swell of her breast. Soon she felt his hot breath only a scant inch from her nipple.

She drew in a deep, silent breath, every muscle in her body tense as she waited for him to make some kind of contact—any kind of contact. He still held her wrists at her sides, and her hands slowly tightened into fists. Almost involuntarily she leaned toward him, seeking his mouth, pressing forward in small increments, until finally her nipple grazed his lips in the tiniest whisper of a touch.

"That's right, baby," he whispered. "Come to me."

She leaned in more, and an instant later she felt his tongue. Hot. Wet. Teasing her nipple, back and forth, over and over, until she felt as if it was on fire.

Oh, *yes*.

He moved to her other breast, giving it the same treatment, moving his tongue against her hardened nipple in gentle, mesmerizing strokes. Her eyes drifted closed as he continued to hold her hands at her sides, touching her only with his mouth. She'd never felt anything like it in her life.

Then slowly he worked his way back up, kissing as he went. At the same time, he slid his hands up her arms, until finally he was holding her face and kissing her deeply. She placed her palms against his chest, then eased her arms around his neck.

It felt good. *So good.*

Then he stopped. Let go of her. Backed away.

Her eyes sprang open. "Jack?"

She heard repeated soft thuds of something hitting the floor. Then he swept her up into his arms abruptly and lowered her to the ground onto something soft. Towels. Sheets. Linens that had been on the shelves only a moment before were now heaped on the floor, cradling her like a cloud. The scent of laundry detergent and fabric softener filled her nose.

Before she could open her mouth to protest, he covered

it with a kiss, a deep, hard, insistent kiss that didn't even allow her to come up for air. By the time he finally pulled away, she was nearly gasping, barely aware of him pulling off her boots. He tossed them aside, then skimmed his hands back up her legs to her thighs and then to her waist, where he hooked his fingers beneath the waistband of her pants and pulled them off.

She gasped at the feeling of being suddenly naked, particularly when she realized that he'd taken her panties right along with her pants. He tossed them both aside. She fumbled for a towel and yanked it over her, but he pushed it away.

"No. I want you naked."

"For God's sake, Jack. We're in a linen closet!"

"What tipped you off? The towels and sheets?"

"If somebody has a key—"

"My foot's right against the door. I promise you I won't let anybody in."

"But—"

"Trust me, sweetheart. I've got everything under control." He settled down beside her once again, splaying his palm against her stomach, then moved his hand up to caress her breast. "And I mean *everything*."

"But—but I'm naked, and you're not even—"

He began kissing her again, his fingers cupping her breast, then finding her nipple and pinching it gently between his fingers.

"Is this what they felt like last night?" he murmured against her lips. "Hard? Tight?"

She felt a shot of pure lust that seemed to pool right between her legs. *Yes. Exactly.*

To her surprise, she felt alive in a way she'd never felt before, terrified that somebody was going to come through that door at the same time she was desperate for Jack to continue touching her.

He teased his fingertips over both her breasts, following his touch with kisses, then stroked his hand down her rib cage to her waist. The air in the closet was cool, and she felt goose bumps rise on her flesh even though his hand felt sizzling hot.

"Last night," he whispered. "In bed. Did you do what I told you to?"

Her heart lurched.

"Did you?"

She paused, saying the word on a whispered breath. "Yes."

"Did you think about me touching you instead?"

"Jack—"

"Just answer me."

She exhaled. "Yes."

"Would you have let me?"

"I—I don't know."

He placed his hand just above her knee, then inched it slowly up her thigh.

"Will you let me now?"

The word *no* tried to form in her mind, but it never quite came together. Mindlessly she let her knees part. Jack slid his hand between her thighs, finding the moist folds there. He slipped a finger inside her, and she felt a rush of unbelievable pleasure.

"Oh, baby. You must have felt just like this last night. Hot and wet."

He swirled his fingertips around her clitoris, then stroked it softly.

"Is this what you were thinking about? Me touching you like this?"

Yes, oh yes, oh yes...

"I wanted to come to your bed last night," he whispered.

Her heart jolted. "Why didn't you?"

"Because if you'd told me no, I wouldn't have been able to stand it."

He continued to stroke her, and soon Rachel was lost in the feeling, not sure she could have come back to reality even if she'd wanted to.

"Is that what you would have done?" Jack said. "Would you have told me no?"

"I don't know," she said breathlessly. "Maybe."

He tucked his other hand beneath her neck and kissed her lips, her cheek, then whispered into the hollow of her neck. "And maybe not?"

"Maybe...not."

She clutched his shoulder, then pulled his sweater tightly into her fist. Her breathing became harsh, and as the flame inside her grew brighter, she couldn't stop herself from rocking her hips to meet his strokes.

She reached for his belt buckle. "Jack," she said, barely able to speak. "Take something off."

She tried to shift her hips to one side, but he followed along, continuing to drive her right to the brink.

"Jack...*please*," she said, her breath coming in short spurts. "I want you...with me..."

But then the thought was lost, because she was close, so close. She groaned. *No!* She wanted to feel him inside her. Now. She wanted to...

And then she couldn't argue anymore, couldn't speak, couldn't do anything but give herself to Jack, aware of nothing else on earth but the feeling of his hands, his lips, his all-consuming presence taking her higher and higher...

"Let go, baby," he murmured against her ear. "Just let go..."

Her body tensed. She clamped her hand onto Jack's arm and arched against him. She gasped once, twice, and all at once it was if something exploded inside her, sending a white-hot rush of pleasure shooting through her like a rocket. No noise, she told herself, afraid somebody might hear, but even though she bit her lip, a cry still escaped, and Jack covered her mouth with his, muffling the sound with a deep, soul-shattering kiss. He continued to stroke her as wave after wave of hot, intense feeling washed over her, and for several long, electrifying seconds, she knew nothing on earth but his hands, his mouth, and the incredible sensations he released in her. Slowly, slowly, she spiraled downward, the last remnants of her climax pulsing away. But even as it faded, she felt a desperate need to feel Jack on top of her, filling her completely, reaching for the same kind of pleasure he'd just given her.

She reached for his belt again. "Jack. Now. *Please*."

To her immense relief, he slipped from her grasp and moved away. She saw him rise to his knees, then to his feet, and it was all she could do not to reach up and rip his jeans off before he could accomplish the task himself.

Then, to her surprise, he turned away.

"Jack?"

She could just barely make out his silhouette as he moved through the darkness. In the next moment, to her complete horror, he unlocked the door and opened it, spilling a shaft of light from the hall into the room. She gasped and grabbed for a towel, holding it up in front of her. He pulled something from his pocket, lay it on the shelf beside the door, then slipped out and closed the door behind him, plunging the room into darkness once again.

She scrambled to her feet. How could he just *leave* like that?

And—oh, God—where were her clothes?

She moved carefully toward the door and felt for the light switch. She couldn't find it. She turned around and dropped to her knees, the crack under the door providing just enough light that she managed to find her pants. She stood up and yanked them on, then hunted around again and located her bra and sweater. She wiggled into them, sure that at any moment somebody was going to come through that door, and it wouldn't be Jack.

What in the world had she just done? More to the point, what had *he* done?

He'd made a fool out of her. Right now he was probably laughing to himself about how easily he'd managed to get her naked and take her to heaven without removing a stitch of clothing himself. She'd professed over and over that she didn't want him to touch her like this, and yet with little more than a crook of his finger, he'd managed to show her just how easily he could get her to succumb to a little hot sex all over again.

She felt like a fool. *A fool.*

She had to get out of this closet. *Now.* But what did she look like? Her cheeks had to be flushed. Her hair mussed. She might as well have big neon letters scrolling across her forehead: *I just had an orgasm in a linen closet.*

She put her hand on the doorknob. What if somebody saw her come out?

Act nonchalant. As if you're coming out of the bathroom or something. As if you're supposed to be in here.

She swung the door open. Jack was standing right beside it.

It shocked her so much that for a split second she just stood there, staring at him. Then she slid out of the closet and started down the hall.

Jack grabbed her by the arm and spun her around. "Hey, wait a minute! Where are you going?"

"That was a rotten thing to do," she whispered harshly.

"Rotten?" he said incredulously. "I thought it was pretty incredible."

"Yeah. For me."

"For both of us."

"If that's true," she whispered, "they why was I the only one in there stark naked?"

For the first time, she realized that he was every bit as hot and flushed as she was. "I'm a real spur-of-the-moment kind of guy," he said, "but I'm beginning to believe that there are advantages to planning ahead."

"Planning ahead?"

"I didn't have any protection."

Rachel blinked with surprise. "That's why you left?"

"Sweetheart, if I'd stayed in that closet one more minute..." He let out a breath of frustration. "Well, there was no telling what I might have done."

Suddenly she realized that he wasn't trying to get the upper hand. He wasn't trying to play games. He wasn't trying to prove she was a hypocrite. He wanted her just as much as she wanted him, and that was saying a lot. He'd taken her to the height of sexual pleasure only three minutes ago, but already she wanted more of him. *All* of him.

She looked over her shoulder down the hall and saw that they were still alone. She inched closer to him.

"Did you mean that you don't have any protection with you anywhere, or just here?"

"Just here."

She lowered her voice. "So if we were to go back to our room..."

"Yes?"

"We'd be...safe?"

"Yes."

"Then let's go back to our room."

Jack's eyes widened. "Are you sure about that?"

"Would you rather go back to the party?"

"God, no."

He grabbed her hand and led her out into the lobby. They hurried to the elevators, slipping inside an empty one just as the doors were closing.

As the elevator ascended, Jack grabbed her and kissed her, and she curled her arms around his neck, opening her mouth to his, their tongues tangling together. She felt his erection hard against her abdomen, letting her know just how much he wanted her, and that knowledge was enough to send her senses spinning into orbit all over again. With his body still pressed intimately against hers, he pulled away from her lips and she felt the hot rush of his breath against her ear.

"Now, I'm warning you. When we get there, I don't want you changing your mind. I don't want to hear that 'no touching in our room' thing again. If that's the way it's going to be, tell me now. I mean it. Say so right now so I can go outside and throw myself into a snowbank, because believe me, sweetheart, that's exactly what it would take to put out the fire."

"Forget the snowbank," Rachel said. "I'll put out the fire."

11

THE SECOND THE ELEVATOR arrived on the fourth floor, Jack took Rachel by the hand and they hurried down the hall toward their room. At the door, he fumbled through his pocket for the key.

"Hurry," Rachel said.

He had a sudden flashback to their night in San Antonio, and he only hoped he'd be able to get her into the room before he tore her clothes off all over again. He missed the key slot the first time, but finally he managed to open the door. He dragged her inside, threw the key on the floor, then slammed the door and backed her up against it.

"Six months I've been waiting to make love to you again," he said, his voice tight with need. "Six months..."

He grabbed her sweater by the hem and yanked it upward. She was right there with him, pulling and tugging until it slipped off over her head. Then her hands went to his sweater, but he was halfway off with it already. He slung it to the floor, then grabbed his T-shirt by the back of the collar and yanked that off, too.

Kissing her urgently, he unhooked her bra and pushed it away. He swept his hands over her breasts. *Yes*. This was how it had been before, and how he wanted it now—hot and hard and fast and exciting. She was his again. He didn't know what tomorrow would bring, but at least for now she was *his*.

"You made a mess in that linen closet," she said, breathing hard. "The maid is going to hate you."

"Not when she finds the twenty-dollar tip."

"Is that what you left on the shelf beside the door?"

"Yeah. Think I should have left more?"

She laughed. "You're incredible."

"Is that 'good' incredible, or 'bad' incredible?"

"Oh, it's good. It's very, *very* good."

She wrapped her arms around his neck in a possessive grip, her skin hot against his, her scent intensely female. He reached for her breasts again, pressing his hand into the silky flesh, then working outward until he caught a nipple between his fingertips. She arched against him, threading her fingers through his hair.

"Yes," she murmured, dropping her head back against the door. He moved to the other breast, taking it in his mouth, loving the way her nipple tightened beneath his tongue. She dug her fingertips into his shoulders, her breath coming faster and faster.

Suddenly she was pulling him up again. "Kiss me," she said, and she closed her mouth over his, sweeping her tongue against his in a way that drew the breath right out of his lungs. This was exactly how she'd been in San Antonio—hot and ready and demanding—and he loved every minute of it.

Without breaking the kiss, he guided her to the bed, then hooked his foot around her ankle, knocking her off balance. She fell back onto the bed with a surprised expression.

"Sorry, sweetheart," he said, "it's got to be now."

She smiled up at him. "Then get on with it."

The expression on her face and the laughter in her voice were an aphrodisiac like no other. This was what he'd

wanted so badly to see. Her enjoying herself. Enjoying
him.

He skimmed his hands down her sides to the waistband of her pants. "Just thought I'd let you know that
once I get you naked, you're not getting dressed again."

"Ever?"

"Ever."

"But that means I can never leave this room."

"You catch on fast. We've got everything we need right
here. A king-size bed, a fireplace, a huge tub, room service. All the essentials." He hooked his fingers into her
pants, easing them downward. "We can spend the rest of
our lives doing nothing but eating, sleeping and—"

"Jack!"

"What?"

"Stop!"

"What?"

Rachel grabbed his hands and stilled them, a look of ab-
ject shock on her face. Then she yanked herself away from
him, rose to a sitting position and flipped the waistband
of her pants down.

"Oh, no," she repeated. "I don't believe this!"

"What?" Jack said, his heart racing. *"What?"*

"My panties!" she said, her voice low and horrified. "I
left them in the linen closet!"

Jack let out a breath of relief. "Is that all?"

"What do you mean, is that all?"

"Good Lord, Rachel, you scared me to death! I thought
something was really wrong!"

"There *is* something really wrong! I dressed so
quickly...I was so desperate to put something on that I
didn't even realize..."

"Forget about it. I'll buy you a new pair. Hell, I'll buy

you a dozen new pair, as long as you don't mind black lace."

"Jack! Don't you understand? I left my panties in a public place!"

"And I thank you for that," he said. "One less thing for me to take off."

"What if somebody finds them?"

"What if they do?"

"Jack!"

"Are they going to DNA test everyone in the hotel to find out whose they are? Then get on the loudspeaker? 'Rachel Westover, please report to the front desk. We have your panties'?"

"Jack—"

"Don't tell me. It's a sentimental thing. They belonged to your grandmother."

"Will you stop it? This isn't funny!"

He tried suppressing his grin, but he wasn't having a whole lot of luck. "No, actually it *is* funny. It really is. You're just not seeing the humor right now. But if you think about it—"

"Do you have to make a joke about everything?"

"I just don't see the big deal, that's all."

She looked at him with exasperation. "Is there anything that embarrasses you? Anything?"

He just shrugged.

"That's what I thought."

"Will you forget about the panties, already? We were having a good time, Rachel. Don't let something like this ruin things."

She stood up suddenly and retrieved her bra from the floor.

"Hey! What are you doing?"

"Getting dressed."

Jack slumped with frustration. "Rachel, come on!"

She put the bra on quickly, then reached for her sweater and pulled it over her head. "I can't believe I let you do this to me."

"Do what to you?"

"Every time I'm around you, I do dumb, irresponsible, dangerous things!"

"Dangerous?"

"I'm here on business, Jack!"

"What we do behind closed doors is the only business I'm interested in."

"My point exactly. You want sex. You don't give a damn if you ruin my career to get it."

He looked at her, dumbfounded. "Would you explain to me how leaving your panties in a linen closet translates to your career going up in smoke?"

"It's what you do to me! You make me crazy! I can't believe I did that. I just can't believe it!"

She flipped her hair out of the neck of her sweater and started for the door. He stood quickly, caught her by the arm and turned her around.

"Hold on a minute! Where are you going?"

"Back to that linen closet!"

He bowed his head with a sigh of defeat. "Just stay here," he told her. "I'll get your panties."

"But—"

"If you get caught, you won't be able to cover for it." He scooped his T-shirt off the floor and pulled it on. "You'll just stand there with your panties in your hand looking guilty."

"What if the maid's already been in there?" Rachel asked. "What if—"

"Will you stop with the what-ifs? I told you I'd take care of it, and I will."

"If I hadn't done this in the first place, there wouldn't be anything to take care of."

"Enough, okay? I get the picture. It was a mistake. You never should have done it. You didn't enjoy it in the least. Does that about sum it up?"

Jack pulled his sweater on, hating the regret he heard in her voice. What had happened between them tonight had been pretty damned good, and if only they hadn't gotten sidetracked, it could have been downright explosive. She didn't see it that way, though. She saw it as some stupid, misguided indiscretion, just as she'd seen their night together in San Antonio.

"I'll be back in a few minutes," he told her.

He yanked the door open and left the room, striding down the hall with a hard-on that made walking just slightly short of impossible. How had this happened? How could he be on the verge of hot sex one moment and be hunting down a pair of rogue panties the next?

He punched the button for the elevator. Three times. *Hard.* Hell, he didn't want to make love to her. What had he been thinking? Late-night search and retrieval. That was what he really wanted to do.

Right after he threw himself into a snowbank.

THE NEXT MORNING, JACK SAT down at a table in the main restaurant of the hotel, where a huge buffet of made-to-order omelets, hash browns, sausage, bacon, bagels and every other breakfast food imaginable awaited hungry guests. And he didn't feel like eating a thing.

He sipped a cup of coffee, staring down at the newspaper in front of him. If it had been printed in Russian, he wouldn't have known the difference, and for all he was paying attention, the coffee could have been motor oil.

Last night he'd gotten Rachel's panties, come back to

their room, tossed them at the foot of her bed, then slept on the sofa because he was pretty damned sure she didn't want him in her bed. Not exactly the kind of evening he'd had in mind when they'd rushed up the elevator, so hot for each other they were lucky they hadn't set the building on fire.

When he woke up half an hour ago, he'd asked Rachel if she was coming down for breakfast, and she'd told him to go on without her. She wouldn't even look at him. So he'd taken a shower, dressed, then come downstairs by himself.

He'd already reached the conclusion that he'd gone too far too fast last night. Dragging Rachel into that linen closet had seemed like a great idea at the time, but when it got right down to it, sex in a semipublic place was something that the average person really ought to work their way up to, much less a person as self-conscious as she was.

And that really was the key, after all. He thought panties left in a linen closet to be no big deal, and she thought it warranted a red alert. Just when he thought that maybe the two of them were absolutely perfect for each other, something happened to remind him of just how different they really were.

On the surface, anyway.

God, he hated this. Why did she have to be so uptight, when he knew that deep down she really wanted to let loose?

You're a glutton for punishment.

He was beginning to believe that. He was just like a miner who saw a tiny vein of silver, then obsessed over the possibility of uncovering a spectacular find. Just when he told himself that it wasn't worth it, that *she* wasn't worth it, he'd think again about how she'd saved that

mall atrium from the atrocities of modern design. He'd
think about the smiles she gave him sometimes, the genuine ones that seemed to open up her face and let him see
right inside her. And then he'd think about the look of
sexual excitement in her eyes every time she gave in to her
desires.

That was all it took. Those tiny, mesmerizing moments
kept him coming back for more, kept him in search of the
woman he knew she was hiding inside. Still, though, he
knew that some miners spent their whole lives looking for
that big strike, enticed by that little bit of glitter, and never
found it. The way things were going right now, he was
destined to be just one more dreamer.

He sighed. Right now he just wanted to get her to speak
to him again.

"Hey, Jack."

He looked up to see Megan standing beside his table.
Her red hair clashed wildly with the hot-pink sweater she
wore. Its hem barely grazed the low-slung waistband of
her jeans, offering an occasional glimpse of a gold navel
ring. She slid into the chair opposite him, laying down the
pile of brochures she'd been holding on the table in front
of her.

"Where's Rachel?"

"Sleeping in."

Megan eyed him carefully. "And she's letting you run
loose all by yourself?"

"She has no idea where I am."

"Uh-oh. Trouble in paradise?"

Jack sighed. "You might say that."

"You sure looked like you were getting along last
night."

"We were. To a point."

"You want to tell me about it?"

He laughed humorlessly. "Better not."

"So she's mad at you?"

"Oh, yeah."

Megan nodded. "Wow. That's too bad. I guess this kinda puts a kink in your plans, huh?"

"Looks like it."

"Well, you don't strike me as the kind of guy who goes down without a fight. So what are you going to do to fix things?"

"Haven't decided yet. I have a feeling that she's not going to want to have much to do with me today. In fact, I doubt she'll even come out of our room. And if I go back there, we'll probably just get into a fight all over again."

"Then let's find a way to get her out of your room. She can't yell at you in front of other people."

"Short of setting off the fire alarm, that's going to be a tough thing to do." He motioned to the pile of brochures. "What are those?"

Megan shrugged. "It's a little boring around here. I got these from the front desk. Stuff to do around Silver Springs."

One of the brochures caught his attention and he slid it out of the pile. He opened it up, and a plan began to form in his mind.

He looked up at Megan. "Does your offer to help still stand?"

She smiled. "You bet. Anything to stir up a little excitement around here."

Jack leaned his forearms on the table and dropped his voice.

"Okay, here's what I want you to do..."

RACHEL LAY IN BED, staring at the ceiling, still feeling painfully embarrassed over what had happened last night. But that didn't mean she wasn't starting to feel a little silly at the same time.

Jack had asked her if she wanted to go to breakfast, and she couldn't even look at him when she told him to go on without her. Funny enough, it wasn't because she was angry with him. It was because she was starting to feel as if maybe—just maybe—she'd overreacted a teensy little bit.

All right, she'd overreacted a lot. But that didn't change the fact that she did crazy things whenever she was around Jack. Things that were totally out of character. Things that were sure to get her into some kind of trouble before this retreat was over.

Yes, she loved being with him. But Jack was like chocolate and fine food and vintage wine and all those other wonderful temptations that drew her like magnets. A little taste was wonderful, but indulging in too much of any of them, Jack included, and she'd pay the price forever. Logically she knew that was true.

God, she was beginning to hate logic.

Suddenly there was a knock at the door. Rachel threw on her robe, went to the door and peered out the peephole.

Megan?

She opened the door. Megan swept into the room, then stopped short and looked at Rachel.

"Love the robe," she said.

Rachel slumped with resignation. Okay, that was it. It was time for some new loungewear.

"Megan? What do you want?"

"I ran into Jack downstairs."

"You did?"

"We had breakfast together. He told me he had some business to take care of this morning, so you'd be by yourself." She handed Rachel a brochure. "He told me that you might be interested in this."

Rachel glanced at the brochure. "A walking tour of downtown Silver Springs?"

"Yeah. Do you want to come with me?"

"With you? You mean, just the two of us?"

"Sure."

"On an historical tour?"

"Yeah. Why not?"

"Because you've never struck me as the type who'd actually enjoy hearing about nineteenth-century history."

"Hey, what are you talking about? I love history! I watch the History Channel all the time!"

"Which programs?"

Megan froze. "Programs? Uh...you know. The...historical ones."

Rachel gave her a skeptical look. "Megan? What's up?"

"Oh, all right!" She rolled her eyes with disgust. "I'll tell you the truth." She leaned in closer to Rachel. "See, somebody told me that the guy who leads the tour is a gorgeous downhill skier who's training for the Olympics. I haven't met a decent guy in this place yet, so I thought maybe if I went on the tour, I could...you know." She wiggled her eyebrows. "Get up close and personal with him."

Now *that* sounded like Megan.

"So why don't you just go on the tour by yourself?" Rachel said. "You don't need me."

"Because I don't want to go by myself."

"I'm sure you can find somebody else to go with you."

"But I want you to come with me."

"Why?"

"Why?" Megan paused. "Well, because."

"Because I'm such wonderful company?"

"Yeah. Of course."

Rachel continued to stare at her pointedly.

"Oh, all right! You could leave me just a little pretense here, couldn't you?" Megan huffed with disgust. "You know all about the history stuff, right? So while we're on the tour, you can feed me intelligent-sounding questions that I can ask Mr. Gorgeous so it'll seem like I'm really interested and he'll think we have something in common. An icebreaker, you know?"

She did. It was exactly what had broken the ice between her and Jack in San Antonio, not that he wouldn't have smashed his way through it under any circumstances. But even with an icebreaker, it wouldn't take Megan's target long to figure out that she'd be lucky to name the last five presidents, even out of order. But then again, she didn't think Megan was after a meaningful, long-lasting relationship based on mutual interests.

"So do you want to go, or not?" Megan asked.

Rachel sighed. She wanted to go on the tour, but she couldn't help thinking how much nicer it would be if it was Jack she was going with, since she knew he'd appreciate it far more than Megan ever would. She didn't know if he was still angry about last night, but whatever the case, since he'd told Megan to invite her on this tour, he clearly had no intention of interacting with her anytime soon. And it had become painfully clear he was going to do exactly what he wanted to do when he wanted to do it. Since there was nothing she could do about that, she decided she might as well go see the sights.

"Sure," she said. "I'll go."

Megan beamed. "Good. I already got the tickets from the front desk at the hotel. The tour's at ten-thirty. Why don't you get dressed and meet me in the lobby at ten?"

AT TEN-TWENTY, RACHEL pulled her car into a parking space on Main Street in downtown Silver Springs. The day was heavily overcast, with shifting winds that spun snowflakes in tight little swirls along the sidewalk. The snowfall was predicted to grow heavier by midafternoon, dropping at least another couple of inches onto the already snow-packed streets.

She and Megan got out of the car. Megan's gaze circled the area. "Wow. Everything sure is old around here, isn't it?"

Yes, time appeared to have come to a complete halt here for approximately the last hundred years. To Rachel, though, it was picture-postcard perfect. Charming. Romantic, even. And she knew Jack would agree.

No. Get him out of your mind. Do you want to be forgetting your panties in public places from now on?

She and Megan crossed the street and had just about reached the door of the tour office, when Rachel heard somebody call her name. She ground to a quick halt and spun around.

Jack was standing behind her.

"Jack?" She shifted her gaze quickly to Megan, then back to him. "What are you doing here?"

"Coming on the tour with you, I hope."

"Don't you have...business to take care of?"

"Yes. You're looking at it."

Rachel had no idea what was going on here, but she certainly couldn't act as if something was wrong. She turned to Megan with a shaky smile. "Well. It appears that Jack can't make up his mind what he wants to do this morning. You don't mind if he joins us, do you?"

"Megan knows," Jack said. "About us."

"She *what?*"

Rachel turned back to Megan, who nodded, and Rachel's stomach dropped to her toes. Oh, God. This couldn't be happening. Expecting Megan not to talk about this was like expecting the sun not to rise in the east.

"She figured it out yesterday at lunch while you were busy in the ladies' room," Jack said. "She pointed out that if I'd been wearing a wedding ring in South America near the equator, I'd have a tan line around my finger."

"I don't believe this," Rachel said.

"Come on, Rachel," Megan said. "There's no reason to go nuts. I swear I'm not going to give away your secret. Actually I'm kind of impressed that you came up with the imaginary husband thing in the first place. Makes me think that deep down, in some small corner of this universe, you and I just might have something in common."

At that moment Rachel knew for sure that she was in big trouble. First Jack had her doing the craziest things she'd ever done in her life, and now Megan was saying that the two of them actually had something in common. What could possibly be next?

"You don't really want to go on this tour, do you?" she asked Megan.

"Uh...no."

"So that story you gave me about the Olympic skier—"

"Bogus. But please don't be mad. I don't know exactly what's wrong between you and Jack. I just know that he wants to make things right again."

She slid the two tickets for the tour into Rachel's hand, then leaned in and whispered in her ear. "Give the guy a chance, will you? He's crazy about you."

With that, she backed away, then turned and trotted down the sidewalk, hailing a cab at the curb.

Rachel stood there, dumbfounded. Slowly she turned to Jack. "She figured it out from a *tan line?*"

"Sharp girl. And believe me, after that, there was no more lying to her. I had no choice but to spill the truth."

"And then you two conspired to get me to go on this tour? Why?"

"Look," he said. "I know I've really set myself up for a fall here. I didn't tell you right away about Megan, and now I've tricked you into coming here. But it's only because I couldn't stand to leave things between us the way they were last night. I tried to talk to you this morning, but you refused even to come to breakfast, and...well, I just didn't know what else to do."

She wanted to be mad at him. She really did. But he was looking at her with such a hopeful expression that her heart began to melt.

The worst had happened. Somebody had discovered her lie. But for some reason, she was focused less on the trauma of being discovered than she was on the words Megan had whispered into her ear.

Give the guy a chance, will you? He's crazy about you.

"Jack?"

"Yeah?"

"You went to all this trouble just to get us talking again?"

"Yeah. Only now I'm thinking it was a really big mistake." He sighed. "I pushed too hard last night, Rachel. Dragging you into a linen closet." He shook his head. "God, what was I thinking?"

She smiled. "Nothing I hadn't been thinking."

"Oh, yeah?"

"Yeah." She stuffed her hands more deeply into her coat pockets. "You could have just come back up to the room this morning if you wanted to talk."

"I thought I stood a better chance if I got you out here, doing something we both love to do."

"I'm glad you did."

He smiled. She sensed the relief he felt, and her heart melted a little more.

"Last night," she said, "thank you for retrieving my..." She looked left and right, then whispered, "Garment."

Jack smiled. "My pleasure."

No. Last night had been her pleasure. All hers. He'd been left out in the cold, so to speak, not once last night, but twice, and suddenly she felt truly sorry about that.

"The snowbank," she said. "Was it...cold?"

His expression became pained. "Well, I did get a few funny looks as I was rolling around in the snow, let me tell you."

"You mean, you actually—"

He raised an eyebrow.

She closed her eyes. "Okay, I know. Stop taking everything you say seriously."

"Not everything," he said, edging closer to her. "You can take this seriously. I want to spend time with you. I want to see where this might lead. I want to forget about all the things that have gone wrong since we've been here and focus on the things that have gone right."

Suddenly Rachel wanted that, too. More than anything.

"And I don't want you to worry about Megan," Jack said. "She told me she won't say a word, and I believe her."

Rachel looked up at him. "I believe her, too."

They stood there staring at each other a long time, the smile on Jack's face melting that last little bit of her heart. Then she heard bells against glass, and she turned to see a man coming out the door of the tour office, and Rachel noticed that about a dozen other people had gathered with them on the sidewalk.

"Is everybody ready to go?" the man said.

"So," Jack said. "I guess we're taking the tour?"

"I have a confession to make."

"Yeah?"

"When I thought I was going with Megan, I wished I was going with you."

Jack took her gloved hand in his. "Then let's go."

12

SILVER SPRINGS WAS an incredible town with an incredible history, and over the next two hours, Jack and Rachel strolled along with the tour guide, inhaling the sights as they huddled close together against the winter breeze. The tiny silver mining town had gone from boom to bust, but still it managed to survive to the current day with most of the downtown area still intact. Along Main Street was a beautiful old church with a steeple that was a masterpiece of intricate carpentry, and beside that was a drugstore built of sandstone and brick in the Romanesque style. They browsed through a small museum with memorabilia from the silver-rush days, then bought fudge at a candy store that supposedly had been open continuously since 1888.

The tour came to an end at the Blythe Hotel, a four-story redbrick structure with narrow arched windows and hand-painted Persian glass accents. They had lunch as a group in the small but elegant Delaware Room, and when the tour finally broke up around one o'clock, Jack and Rachel decided to stay for a while. They went into the lounge, where they sat at a table near the fireplace in leather-bound chairs, sipped coffee and watched the snow fall.

As they sat there, time seemed to slow to a pleasant crawl. The fire was warm, and just looking at Jack warmed Rachel up even more. Because of the heat from the fire, he'd shoved the sleeves of his sweater to his elbows. She stared at his strong forearms with their light covering of golden hair, then let her gaze slide down to his hands—big, dexterous hands that could be both powerfully demanding and softly seductive. His voice was animated, his laughter low and engaging, and right now, as they sat in this beautiful old hotel which they both loved, it seemed that nothing on earth could possibly come between them.

But Rachel knew why she felt that way. Sitting here right now, her job wasn't an issue, his off-the-wall personality wasn't an issue, and the great big lie she'd told about him being her husband wasn't an issue. In a few short days, though, reality would settle in again, and all those things that didn't matter at this moment would matter very much indeed.

She ran her fingertip along Jack's wrist, and he took her hand in his.

"I really am sorry about last night," she told him. "You were right. It was no big deal. Nobody would have known the panties were mine. But just the thought of it—"

"Then don't think about it."

She sighed. "If you only knew how hard that was."

"It doesn't have to be."

"It does when you were raised the way I was raised."

"What does your upbringing have to do with leaving panties in linen closets?"

She smiled. "Are you kidding? It's the kind of thing that would make my parents disown me. And I'm not being completely facetious about that."

"So your parents are a little uptight."

She laughed. "That's putting it mildly."

"What do they do for a living?"

"My mother's a lawyer. My father's an architect."

"Ah, your father's an architect. You're an architect. Coincidence?"

Rachel thought about that for a long time, running her fingertip over the rim of her cup. She'd told herself since the time she was in high school that it was her career of choice, but it hadn't been her choice at all.

"Actually," she said, "once when I was in high school, I had a momentary bout of insanity and told my parents I wanted to be a history teacher."

"Oh, really? What did they say?"

"They didn't have to say anything. Just the looks on their faces would have been enough for me never to mention it again. They gave me that patented look of theirs, the one that said, 'You're just like your sister—heading down the path to nowhere.'"

"Your sister?"

"Yeah. She's five years older than I am. She went to the same private school I did, only she got lousy grades and thumbed her nose at everything our parents ever tried to do for her." Rachel shook her head. "Instead of going to college, she ran off and eloped. I sincerely thought my mother was going to have a stroke. Of course, that marriage lasted exactly nine months, and she was off with some other guy. Last I heard, she was on husband number three."

"Big disappointment to your parents, huh?"

"Understatement. I still remember those stone-cold looks of disapproval they used to give her." Rachel actually shivered. "The very thought that they'd ever look at me like that froze me right to the bone."

"Like the way they looked at you when you said you were thinking about being a history teacher."

"Pretty much. But most of the time they were telling

me, 'Thank God for you, Rachel. At least you have a head on your shoulders.'" She laughed a little. "I grew up thinking that having a head on your shoulders was one of the most worthwhile things to aspire to."

He grinned. "It shows."

"Yeah, I know," she said with a sigh. "But with luck, maybe sometime in the far, far future, I might actually be able to lighten up and, you know, wear pink, or something."

Jack laughed. "Sweet, nurturing parents, guiding their children into adulthood with all the subtlety of bulldozers."

"That about sums it up. My feelings were always the last thing on the list. 'Don't want to take advance placement courses? Too bad. Take them anyway. They'll put you ahead in college. Don't want to be student council president? Too bad. Run anyway. It'll look good on your college application. Don't want to major in architecture? Too bad. Do it anyway. It's a highly prestigious and lucrative career.' But pretty soon I didn't need them telling me what to do. It got to the point where I did the job for them—'Don't want to work for a company that builds glitzy resorts? Too bad. It's a good career move. Do it, anyway.'"

"So how do you really feel about the buildings you design?"

"Let's just say I'm proud of the creativity I show while staying within the bounds of client preference."

"Like the mall atrium."

"Yes," she said, then frowned. "But even now, when I look at that resort..."

"You wish it wasn't overshadowing a historic little mining town in the heart of the Rocky Mountains."

She sighed. "Yes."

"So you do think that resort is a monstrosity."

"It's hugely profitable...and hideous as it can be. And if you even think of telling anyone I said that, I'll have to kill you."

He smiled. "It appears that your job frustrates you."

"Yes, sometimes it does."

"So quit."

"Oh, please. That's insane."

"There must be a hundred other architecture firms you can work for who think twice before they disfigure the American landscape."

"You're being melodramatic."

"I'm being truthful."

"Maybe. But I can go to the top with this company. I know I can. If Walter puts me in charge of the Reno project, it won't be long before—"

"Before you're at the top of a company that specializes in glass and mirrors and bright lights and glitz when your heart is in Tiffany glass, vintage hardwoods and things that don't glow in the dark. God, Rachel, don't you see what you're doing? You're giving yourself away, piece by piece. Before long there won't be anything left."

She hated what he was saying, because she knew it was true. She'd felt it for some time now, ignoring what was in her heart to pursue success as it had always been laid out to her. Get onto that fast track to the top, and don't get off. For anything.

Or anyone.

"So what about you, Jack?" she said. "Within five minutes of meeting you, women are lusting after you, and men think you're the life of the party. Where did all those people skills come from?"

He raised his eyebrows. "Wow. Didn't know I was so darned impressive."

"Sure you did. You know exactly how you affect people."

He smiled a little, then took a sip of coffee. "Well, when I was growing up, I had to make friends fast, or I'd never have any."

"Why?"

"Because we moved every couple of years. My father is a petroleum engineer. We lived all over the world."

"Where were you born?"

"Houston."

"How many places have you lived?"

"Eight, maybe nine. I'd have to think."

"Domestic, or foreign?"

"Both. Gulf Coast, West Coast, North Sea, Saudi Arabia."

"So where do you call home?"

"What?"

"If you were to say, 'I'm going home for Christmas,' where would home be?"

He shrugged. "My parents live in Malaysia right now. Kuala Lumpur."

"So that's home?"

"Actually, I've never even been there. San Antonio is home now, I guess. I went to college there and stayed."

"But when you were growing up, you lived in a different place every couple of years. It must have been hard trying to make friends."

"Not after I figured out the secret."

"Which was?"

"All I had to do was keep them laughing. Spice things up. I drove the teachers crazy. The other kids loved me."

"Because you drove the teachers crazy."

He laughed. "That was a big part of it."

"It sounds like you had lots of friends. Lots of social life.

I didn't have much of that at all. I spend most of my time with my nose in a textbook."

"Yeah. I guess in a way it was a good thing." Then his smile faded. "But you know, I really envied the kids who'd grown up with each other. Who'd lived in the same neighborhood from the time they were born. Everybody always liked me, but it was hard to make really close friends when you knew you weren't going to be around for long. It was hard to connect to much of anything."

He took a sip of coffee, his face falling into a distinct frown.

"What?" Rachel asked.

"Nothing."

"No, what?"

He laughed a little, but it sounded hollow. "I remember a time when I was ten years old. First day of school in a new town. I walked home after school and forgot where I lived. I couldn't even remember the street name. A lot of the houses in that neighborhood looked alike, and I couldn't tell which one was mine."

"So what did you do?"

"I finally found my way home. I was an hour late, but both my parents were still at work, so nobody knew I'd even been lost. If not for the name on the mailbox, I'd probably still be wandering around that neighborhood."

"God, Jack. That must have been awful."

"Yeah, it was. For the first couple of days when I was in a new place, I felt lost. Alone. Nothing to hold on to. It's a strange feeling when you look at a house and can't even tell if it's the one you live in. But then I'd get used to the new house, make friends and everything would be fine."

"Until the next time you moved."

He stared at her for a moment, then looked away.

"Jack? Why do you volunteer to build those houses in San Antonio?"

He seemed startled by the question. "I don't know, really. I'm good at it, I guess, and it seems like a worthwhile cause."

"Who moves into them?"

"Low-income people who can't afford a down payment. If they're accepted for the program and work for a certain number of hours on their house, and other people's houses, too, they get to move into a home of their own."

"Sounds wonderful."

"It is." A warm smile came over his face. "You should see what happens every time we finish a house. There's this dedication ceremony where all the people on the block come out to officially welcome the new family to the neighborhood. And the kids. They're really something. Up to then, most of them have been shuffled around from one low-income apartment to another, and they get so excited about the new house that's all theirs. Everybody's excited. The sense of community is unbelievable." He paused, as if reflecting on that, an uncharacteristically somber expression coming over his face. "You asked me why I do it. I guess maybe that's why."

"Because you think everybody ought to have a place to call home?"

"Yeah. Maybe so."

They stared at each other a long time, and an understanding passed between them that sent a warm shiver down her spine. There was much more inside this man than she'd ever realized before, and so much more she wanted to find out.

"I drive you crazy, don't I?" Jack said softly.

"What do you mean?"

"Because I never take anything seriously."

"I don't think that's completely true, is it?"

He looked away. "The truth is, Rachel, that while I have hundreds of friends, I don't have many close ones. I know I make a joke out of everything, but that's because, you know, if you keep it light, keep them laughing, when it comes time to say goodbye..."

His voice tapered off, but Rachel knew. She knew what he wasn't saying, maybe better than he knew it himself.

"It doesn't break your heart," she whispered.

He never responded. He just stared down at his coffee cup, and for the first time Rachel saw right through him to the child he must have been, to the vulnerable heart that he hid away behind the jokes and the laughter. She thought about the time they'd spent together in San Antonio, sharing a connection that had gone beyond sexual attraction into something meaningful for both of them. And then she thought about how she'd left him in the middle of the night without even telling him her last name.

"This is a beautiful hotel," she said.

He looked up. "Yes. It is."

"Pretty chandeliers. And I love the oak paneling."

He picked up his coffee cup. "I do, too."

"I wonder what the rooms look like?"

He froze, his cup hovering in midair.

"Do you suppose they have oak paneling, too?" she said.

"Possibly."

"Clawfoot tubs?"

"Maybe."

"Four-poster beds?"

He set his cup back down on the table. "They might."

She smiled. "Would you like to go find out?"

13

JACK PAID THEIR BILL, and he and Rachel walked leisurely to the front desk, checked in, then headed up the elevator. He gave her a kiss as they ascended, a long, leisurely, slow-motion kiss that enveloped them both in a warm, relaxing glow. He had the feeling that the moment was finally just right, as if there were no more games left to play, as if finally they both knew exactly what they wanted.

They came into the room, and it turned out Rachel was right about the four-poster bed. They admired it, along with the light fixtures, the cherry dresser, the crown moldings, the draperies. Jack tossed their coats into a chair in the corner of the room. When he turned back around, Rachel held up her palm.

"Stop right there."

Surprised at her sudden command, he did as she said. She hit the wall switch. Darkness fell over the room. Because the day was so overcast, only a faint glow of light seeped around the edge of the draperies.

"Take off your clothes," she whispered.

"What?"

"You heard me. Right now."

Take off your clothes? Had those words just come out of Rachel's mouth?

He smiled. "I get it. This is payback. For you ending up naked all by yourself in that linen closet."

"Payback?" She laughed softly. "Maybe. I guess you'll find out once your clothes are off, won't you? Now, do it."

He did. In record time. He dragged his T-shirt off right along with his sweater. He unbuckled his belt, then yanked off everything south of his waist in one big swoop, kicking it all aside.

"Your turn," he said.

She laughed again. Softly. Seductively. "Sorry, Jack. That's not how this game is played, is it?"

Jack thought his heart was going to leap right out of his chest. Her voice was hot. Sex-filled. Erotic as hell. He felt himself getting hard just listening to her, followed by a mental flash of what he'd done to her in that linen closet. And what she might be getting ready to do to him.

She walked over and stood in front of him, then lifted her hands to his shoulders. He reached for her.

"Don't move," she said. "Not one muscle."

Impossible. He had one muscle that was moving. In fact, it was growing with every breath he took.

She pushed him backward until he bumped against the wall. With infinite slowness, she ran her hands down his arms to his wrists, then encircled them. He had no idea what she intended to do, but the anticipation was about to kill him.

She kissed him once, gently, then whispered in his ear, "I know what you like."

She did. That night in San Antonio, her learning curve in his class, *Going Wild 101*, had been steep. Very steep. In fact, she'd graduated with honors in a matter of hours.

Apparently she was coming back for postgraduate study.

She teased his earlobe with her tongue, then worked her way back to his mouth, where she kissed him slowly and sensually, heat radiating from her lips to his. He tried to disengage his wrists so he could hold her, but she refused to let go. She continued to kiss him in a way that was warm and sweet and intimate, with no other contact except her mouth against his and her hands around his wrists.

Then, slowly, she pulled away, and sank to her knees in front of him.

Oh, boy. If he'd been hot before, he was on fire now.

She leaned toward him, still holding his wrists, and when he felt her hot breath right at the tip of his penis, his heart rate shot through the roof. He leaned his head back against the wall and closed his eyes. Waiting.

He felt nothing but her breath. Just her breath, in soft, rhythmic exhalations. Finally he strained forward, dying for some kind of contact.

"That's right, baby," she whispered. "Come to me."

He groaned in agony as he heard his own words coming back to haunt him. "See, I told you it was payback."

She laughed, her breath tickling him yet again. "I haven't even begun to pay you back yet."

Then he felt it. Her tongue. Swirling around the tip of his penis.

Oh, yeah.

He tried to reach for her, but she held his wrists firmly at his sides and continued to tease him. The unbelievable sensation of her warm, wet tongue circling around and around the head of his penis, then blazing a trail along its length, was just about more than he could stand. But still she persisted, applying just enough pressure to drive him wild.

Finally she licked her way back to the tip, then closed her mouth over it, applying gentle suction. His entire body went rigid, the rush of pleasure so intense that he almost lost it right there. His breath quickened, his pulse heading for the stratosphere. She tightened her hands against his wrists and leaned into him, taking him in, inch by inch, deeper and deeper, then moving out again, then in, then out, over and over and over...

With a strangled groan, he pulled his wrists free, grabbed her by the upper arms and hauled her to her feet. He turned and pressed her up against the wall, releasing a significant amount of his coiled-up energy in a long, hard, kiss. Finally he pulled away, breathing hard, his lips still grazing hers.

"I wasn't finished," she said.

"Believe me—you were closer to finished than you think."

"But—"

"Playtime's over," he said. "Time to get serious."

"Wait a minute. Did I just hear Jack Kellerman say it was time to get *serious?*"

"Damn right you did."

"Imagine that," she said, as he reached for her shirt buttons. "There really is a first time for everything."

He unfastened one of her shirt buttons, and the next one, then realized his hands were actually trembling. He couldn't believe it. He'd relieved women of their clothing on a regular basis since he was a teenager, yet somehow it felt as if it were the first clumsy time all over again.

He fumbled with the third button, but it refused to budge. After several futile attempts, he bunched the fabric in his fist and rested his forehead against hers, taking a deep, calming breath.

"I'm trying not to tear your shirt. I really am. But these damned buttons—"

To his utter astonishment, she grabbed the sides of the shirt and ripped them apart. Buttons plinked against the hardwood floor.

His eyes flew open wide. "Did you just rip your shirt open?"

She looked down at herself. "Why, look at that. I sure did."

This day just got better and better.

"I'll buy you a new one," he said, sliding his hands inside her shirt and around to the small of her back, pulling her against him until the lace cups of her bra tickled his chest and his erection pressed against her abdomen. "Along with the black lace panties."

"A regular shopping spree."

"Just say the word."

He kissed the hollow of her throat, then moved up the side of her neck, finally taking her earlobe between his teeth, nipping it gently. He pulled her shirttail from her pants, then brought his hands back around and flicked her bra open, sliding it off her shoulders along with her shirt, allowing them both to fall to the floor behind her. She did the same to her pants. When he pulled her back against him, she whispered in his ear.

"You're right. Playtime's over."

She slid from his arms, took him by the hand and led him toward the bed. Then she stopped suddenly and spun around, her hand at her throat.

"Oh, Jack. Please tell me that you brought a condom. Please tell me—"

He silenced her with a quick kiss. "Sweetheart, from now on I wouldn't even think of going out for the morning paper without one."

He grabbed his jeans from the floor, extracted some plastic packets from one of the pockets and tossed them to the bed.

"*Four?*" Rachel said.

"I like to dream big."

She smiled. "Are you planning on using all those?"

"Is that a challenge?"

"Yeah. Think you can rise to it?"

"I think I already have."

She coaxed him to lie back on the bed. She ripped open one of packets and removed the condom. She straddled his thighs, took his penis in her hand, stroking it gently before rolling the condom over it. She followed it slowly all the way down, one hand over the other, until she'd slid it into place. If a man could die of ecstasy, he was certainly in danger of that now.

"Sweetheart," he said a little breathlessly, "you're making me crazy here."

"Oh? Shall I apologize?"

"Apologize?"

"Kiss it and make it better?"

She wrapped her hand around his penis, then lowered her head and kissed the tip. Her hair cascaded over her left cheek like a dark waterfall, tickling his thigh. Another kiss. Then another. He squeezed his eyes closed, trying to hold on, but damn. She was taking him *way* past crazy.

He sat up suddenly and grabbed her by the arms. Pulling her down on top of him, he rolled over, pinning her beneath him.

"I can see I'm going to have to take control of this situation," he said. "You've run amok."

She grinned. "Run amok?"

"Completely."

They stared at each other a long, electrifying moment. She traced her fingertips over his cheek, her blue eyes shimmering in the dim light.

"Make love to me, Jack."

Words he thought he'd never hear again.

He moved between her legs, then rose above her, and

she guided him toward her opening. When he finally slid inside her and her muscles clamped down hard around him, he sucked in a breath and held it, shocked by the unbelievable pleasure of finally being inside her again.

"Oh, baby," he said under his breath. "That's so damned *good.*"

He'd forgotten. He'd forgotten just how incredible it was to be with her like this. He was so far beyond ready for her that it was all he could do to take it easy, take it slow, but then she arched up to meet his strokes, wrapping her legs around him and drawing him in, and he realized that she didn't want it slow, she wanted it *now.* When he thrust harder, she rose to meet him, when he moved faster, so did she. The sensation of her body beneath his, naked and silky and hot and moving with his in perfect rhythm, was all he could ever have asked for. All he would ever ask for, if this woman could be his forever.

Forever.

He heard that word playing over and over in his head, pounding like a drumbeat, telling him his search was over and he'd finally come home.

He kissed her neck and felt her breath against his cheek, and when it turned to short little gasps, he knew she was close. She was tight around him and burning hot, and with her breasts pressed against his chest and her arms wrapped around him and her legs like velvet vises clamped around his hips, he knew he couldn't last much longer.

"Rachel," he whispered. "Baby, I'm close. So close..."

She cried out his name and clutched his shoulders, then she drew in a sharp breath and tightened around him. The moment he felt her start to come, he let himself go, driving wildly, until a hard, shuddering climax rocketed through him that seemed to go on forever. It was a rush of feeling so intense that it literally took his breath away, a release of all the pent-up desire for her that he'd lived with for the past six months. He clamped his arms around her, holding her close, enveloping her body with his until the last ripples of pleasure faded away.

In slow increments, he felt her relax beneath him, her breathing becoming softer and more measured. He moved to lie beside her, then rose on one elbow and stared down at her in the dim light of the hotel room.

"I can't believe I did all that," she said.

He brushed her hair away from her cheek. "You're not getting cold feet on me again, are you?"

"No. It's just so...not me. It's one thing when I'm in the middle of it. I mean, it's..."

"Wonderful? Fun? Exciting?"

"Yes. But then afterward, when I start thinking about it—"

He stroked his hand along her arm. "Then don't think about it. Just feel it."

"That's the part that I'm afraid of," she whispered. "The feeling."

It was then that he knew. It wasn't that she was just uptight or straitlaced. She was afraid—afraid of getting carried away, of being powerless, of something sweeping her away that she couldn't rationalize, couldn't categorize, couldn't pigeonhole into something she could understand and, therefore, control. And it was no wonder. The way she'd been raised, with parents dictating every move she made, doling out approval only when she followed their carefully prescribed path, of course she'd hide her own feelings away and refuse to acknowledge them.

"Is that why you ran out on me in San Antonio?" he asked. "Because you were afraid of what you were feeling?"

"I don't know. Maybe."

"Are you afraid now?"

She paused. "No. But when I get out in the real world again—"

"Sweetheart, what's out there—that's not real. Not when you have to put a different face on to hide who you really are. What's between us—*that's* the real world."

They lay together in silence, a long, comfortable silence they seemed to melt right into.

"Nothing's going on at the resort tonight," Rachel said. "Everybody is on his own."

"Are you thinking we should stay here until tomorrow?"

"That's what I'm thinking."

"We can order room service," he said.

"And make love again."

"And again."

"And again."

Jack tapped his thumb and fingertips together, counting. "Yeah. Three more times. But that's it."

"Why?"

"That's when we run out of condoms."

She smiled. "You do have more at the other hotel for tomorrow, don't you?"

"Oh, yeah. And the whirlpool bath. Don't forget about that."

"Sounds wonderful."

He gave her a kiss, a deep, endless kiss, savoring the richness of the moment, thinking that a trip to heaven itself couldn't match being in this bed with Rachel right now.

But then, out of nowhere, a feeling of apprehension crept in. He tried to brush it away, but it kept coming back, churning through his mind and refusing to go away.

Finally he lay down and pulled Rachel up next to him, cradling her head against his chest.

"Rachel?"

"Yes?"

"When I wake up tomorrow morning, where will you be?"

There was a moment of silence, as if she didn't understand.

"Right here, Jack," she whispered. "Right here with you."

14

WHEN RACHEL BLINKED her eyes open the next morning, she found Jack already awake. He was propped up on one elbow staring down at her, just lying there staring at her, with a glimmer in his green eyes that said he had something important on his mind. He pulled her up next to him, and she felt something pressing on her hip.

"About time you woke up," he said.

She smiled. "Feels like I'm just in time."

Jack threaded his fingers through her hair and kissed her, then made love to her again, slowly, sensually, with a dreamy kind of intimacy that she could have lost herself in forever.

Later, they checked out of the hotel. Rachel hadn't been skiing yet, so in spite of the fact that they were both exhausted, they spent the morning on the slopes, only to return to downtown Silver Springs to have a late lunch at the same tacky little restaurant they'd gone to before. Rachel wisely declined another of the killer drinks, but she did have a basket of curly fries to go with her hamburger, and she couldn't believe how good it all tasted.

Being with Jack was one incredible experience after another, but as the day progressed, she couldn't help the feeling of foreboding that crept in. Their time together was running short, and she had no idea what was going to happen between them after the retreat was over.

As they were finishing lunch, Jack grew quiet. That was

so out of character for him that she knew he must be thinking the same thing she was. The unspoken question hovered between them for several minutes, until finally Jack voiced it.

"Rachel?" he said. "Where do we go from here?"

There it was. And she wished she had an answer. "I don't know. The two of us—"

"Are great together."

"But this isn't real life, Jack."

"Now, what did I tell you about that 'real life' thing?"

"You know what I mean. We're completely different."

"We balance each other," he said.

"We drive each other crazy."

"But it's a good kind of crazy, isn't it?"

"We barely know each other."

His smile faded. "I don't think that's really true, do you?"

She didn't. She could think of men she'd dated for months whom she knew even less about than she did Jack, and with those men, she hadn't even had a desire to know more. With Jack, she wanted to know everything. Even the kinds of things it would take a lifetime to discover.

She couldn't believe it. Was she actually thinking about the possibility of forever with Jack? And could he be thinking the same about her? How could a relationship with him feel so impossible and so right all at the same time?

"We don't have to decide anything right now," she said.

"Come tomorrow, we'll be a thousand miles apart. Do you really want that?"

"I don't know what I want."

"I think you do. I think you know what you want, but

you just don't want to admit it. For God's sake, Rachel, you're eating curly fries."

She smiled. She felt herself falling for this man more with every word he spoke. But where matters of the heart were concerned, she didn't trust her own judgment. She kept thinking there was a punch line in here somewhere. That the joke would be on her. That she'd fall for a man who was exciting and exhilarating and sexy as hell, only to wake up one morning and realize there was a lot more to life than that and she'd made a terrible mistake.

But at this moment, nothing looked so right.

"Tomorrow," she said. "Let's talk about it tomorrow."

Jack acted as if there was plenty more he wanted to say on the subject. Instead he stole a curly fry from her basket.

"Okay," he said. "Tomorrow. I'm going to hold you to that."

He popped the fry into his mouth, then checked his watch. "Did you want to do some more skiing this afternoon?"

"Actually, I was thinking I'd rather go swimming."

"What?"

"In the tub."

Jack smiled. "Sounds good to me."

"Then we have the party tonight. We've been instructed to dress casual and be prepared."

"Ah, yes. I hear Megan has a slate of games lined up for everyone to play."

Rachel closed her eyes. "I can't even imagine what games she's going to come up with. Knowing Megan, they'll be designed to irritate and aggravate."

Jack grinned. "Sounds like my kind of evening."

THAT NIGHT AT EIGHT O'CLOCK, Jack and Rachel entered the ballroom, and instantly people waved and called out to them. Rachel found herself waving and smiling back, and it didn't escape her attention that without Jack's influence over the past three days, she would have slunk into the room, stood at the back and generally offered very little in the way of interaction with her fellow employees. Instead she was actually starting to feel at ease in a crowd—this crowd, anyway—and when she moved next to Jack and he put his arm around her, it felt as natural as anything in her life ever had.

The chairs in the ballroom were arranged for people to be seated as an audience. At the front of the room, next to a podium, Megan was lining up six chairs facing the crowd.

"What do you suppose she's got in store for us?" Rachel asked.

"I don't know," Jack said. "But I can't wait to find out."

Then Megan spotted them and waved. "Jack! Rachel!" She trotted over to them. "Hey, you guys! I need you to do me a favor."

"What's that?" Rachel asked.

"We're going to be playing a game to see how much couples know about each other. I need three couples. I want you to be one of them."

"Us?" Rachel dropped her voice to a whisper. "Megan, you know we can't play a game like that!"

"Sure you can. No big deal. If you get the questions wrong, so what? It's all in fun."

"No," Rachel said. "I don't think that's a good idea."

"Who else is playing?" Jack asked.

"Ronnie and Anne, and Phil and Suzy."

Rachel actually felt the hairs bristle on the back of her neck. "Phil and Suzy are playing?"

"Yeah. Can I count on you guys?"

"Sure," Jack said, giving Megan a look that said, *Don't*

worry, I'll talk her into it. Megan grinned and hurried off, and Rachel felt a swell of apprehension.

"Jack, this is a really bad idea. We're not really married. How are you supposed to be able to answer questions about me?"

"Hey, I know more about you than a lot of other people do. As long as they ask me your favorite sexual position."

"Jack!"

"Will you trust me on this, sweetheart? It's no big deal. Just play along. These people want to see you having a good time. I guarantee you that Walter is looking for a people person for that project manager job. Prove you can take a joke, and it'll go a long way, okay?"

"Joke? What do you mean, joke?" She shook her head, waving her hand. "No. You know I'm no good at this stuff."

He took her by the shoulders. "It's just a matter of loosening up at little. Of not worrying about every word that comes out of your mouth. Of being spontaneous. And hey, I *know* you can be spontaneous."

"With you it's different. With everybody else—"

"I'll help you. Just go with the flow, and it'll be fine, okay?"

Finally Rachel nodded. Maybe Jack was right. It was time she learned to lighten up. Maybe a silly game like this was just what she needed.

Okay. So she didn't really believe that, but it sure made it sound as if she was making progress.

Five minutes later, Megan grabbed the microphone from the podium. She got the group's attention, welcomed them for an evening of fun and games, then launched right in.

"Okay, everybody!" Megan said, in her best emcee voice. "We're going to play a little game to find out how much couples know about each other. Three adventurous couples have volunteered to suffer through—I mean, *play* the game. Will they come up to the front right now?''

Jack took Rachel's hand and they walked up to the front of the room to stand with the other couples. Everybody applauded, with a few whistles thrown in, and Rachel started to get nervous. Very nervous.

"Ladies, I want you to go out into the lobby for a few minutes, where you can't hear the answers your husbands give to some *very* serious questions about you. Then we'll call you back in and see which couple knows each other the best."

Rachel didn't like this. She didn't like the gleam in Megan's eyes, she didn't like the way the audience was already grinning, and most of all, she didn't like the words "some very serious questions" because it was obvious that they weren't going to be serious in the least.

She gave Jack one last please-let-this-be-all-right look as she left the room with Suzy and Anne, and he smiled and winked at her.

They waited in the lobby, making small talk, speculating about the nature of the questions. Rachel had a little anxiety attack going on, but she had to admit that she felt better knowing that Jack was going to be there to cover for her in case she said anything dumb. At the beginning of this retreat, she'd been terrified of every word that came out of his mouth, but in reality, everything he'd said had made her feel more secure, not less. And as sappy as it sounded, just being with him made her feel as if a little sunshine had finally made its way into her life.

Tomorrow it might all be over with.

But did it have to be?

There were so many obstacles in their way, geography being the least of them. When it came right down to it, they were as different as any two people could be, but somehow, in the last few days, she'd started to feel as if they weren't two opposing forces, but two pieces of the same whole.

It seemed as if aeons passed before somebody finally came out and escorted them back to the party. She felt a shot of apprehension as she walked back through the door, but when she took her seat beside Jack, he draped his arm across the back of her chair in a warm, protective gesture, and she knew in her heart that everything was going to be all right. He had a set of cards in his lap that she assumed had his answers to the questions Megan had asked, and the look on his face said he was actually enjoying himself. But from Jack, would she have expected anything less?

"Okay, ladies," Megan said. "Each question is worth five points, with a fifteen-point bonus question at the end. Are you ready?"

They all nodded, and Megan turned to Suzy. "Suzy, you and Phil are sharing a gourmet meal. Which of these four courses will he say that you like the best? The appetizer, main course, side dish, or dessert?"

Suzy said "dessert," and Phil lifted his card to reveal a match. He gave his wife the obligatory peck on the lips, and everybody applauded politely.

"Okay, that's good for five points," Megan said, then offered the question to Anne. She matched Ronnie with "main course." Then everyone turned to Jack and Rachel.

Rachel wasn't sure what to say. Jack knew she was into healthy eating but not heavy eating, but it didn't really matter what she answered. Getting this one wrong would hardly make somebody leap to his feet and accuse him of lying about being her husband.

"Side dish," she said.

Jack flipped his card up to reveal "dessert." Rachel tried to look appropriately disappointed. He gave her a sad face, then turned to the audience. "Actually, Rachel is just being modest. What this woman can do with a can of whipped cream would blow your *mind.*"

The crowd erupted with laughter, and Rachel froze. Jack turned and gave her a quick kiss. "That's okay, sweetheart," he said, loudly enough for the whole room to hear. "You're pretty darned good with the salad tongs, too."

All at once the true nature of the question dawned on her, and her cheeks grew hot with embarrassment. She realized now that there had been a suggestive lilt to Megan's voice as she read the possible answers, indicating that the question could be construed as referring to what might happen after dinner rather than dinner itself. And apparently everyone had realized what was going on but her. Including Jack.

"Next question," Megan said. "Suzy, if you were an Olympic athlete, which sport would your husband say that you would compete in? The hundred-yard dash, the marathon, the high jump or the pole vault?"

Good Lord. From the lilting sound of Megan's voice, she was clearly talking about the Sex Olympics.

Suzy answered "marathon." Phil grinned and flashed his card to show a match, garnering another five points. Ronnie said hundred-yard dash, while Anne went with marathon, so they received no points at all.

"Rachel?" Megan said.

This was awful. No matter what she said, it sounded bad. Just pick one.

"Hundred-yard dash."

Jack slumped with dismay. He turned up his card to reveal "marathon," then leaned toward the audience. "Actually," he said, in a loud stage whisper, pointing at Rachel, "decathlon. *Gold medal.*"

Everybody laughed again, and Rachel felt a shot of total mortification. What was he doing? Making her out to be some kind of sexual maniac?

"Next question," Megan said. "Suzy. Which one of these tools would your husband say that you're the most adept in the use of? Screwdriver, hammer, drill or duct tape?"

Oh, God. Was the sexual innuendo never going to end?

Phil and Suzy missed the question, and so did Ronnie and Anne, because really, what kind of question was it, anyway?

"Okay, Rachel," Megan said. "It's your turn. Screwdriver, hammer, drill or duct tape?"

Since Rachel couldn't bear to say any of the first three, she decided to go with duct tape. Megan had clearly thrown that one in for a laugh, and since it was the funniest response of the four, surely that was the one Jack would go for.

"Duct tape," she said.

Jack grinned, then flipped up his card to reveal "duct tape." Everyone applauded, exaggeratedly so since it was the first question they'd actually gotten right. He gave her a quick kiss.

"I knew we'd match on that one, sweetheart," he said, then turned to the audience. "She used up a whole roll of it after she lost the handcuffs."

Laughter exploded, and the tiny bit of elation Rachel felt at finally getting a question right was washed away by a new wave of humiliation. *Handcuffs?* What was he trying to do to her?

"Next question," Megan said. "Suzy, on average, over the last year, how many times per week will Phil say that the two of you made love? One to two, three to five, six to eight, or 'I've lost count'?"

Rachel felt nauseated, and it was all she could do not to leap up and rush out of the room at such a ridiculously personal question that was absolutely nobody's business. She couldn't even imagine what Jack was going to answer. The other couples managed to get the question right, and Megan turned to Rachel.

"Okay, Rachel. Your turn. What's it going to be? One to two, three to five, six to eight, or 'I've lost count'?"

"One to two," Rachel said, because that sounded reasonable, and she was going to kill Jack if he said anything else. Then Jack flipped up his card, and her worst fears were realized.

"You've lost *count?*" she said incredulously.

"I'm sorry, sweetheart! First I said one to two, just like you did, since I'm out of the country a lot. But then I got to thinking about the last four days, and Megan did say it was an average."

Everybody hooted at that, and Rachel wanted to crawl away somewhere and die. She'd never been so embarrassed in her life. By the time Jack got through with her, everyone was going to think she was a screaming nymphomaniac.

"Okay," Megan said, "here's where we stand. Phil and Suzy have fifteen points, Ronnie and Anne have ten, and Jack and Rachel..." Megan shook her head sadly, making a *tsk-tsk* noise with her tongue. "Only five points. What seems to be the problem?"

The problem is that my "husband" isn't really my husband, and he's embarrassing me to death. That's *the problem.*

"I don't know," Jack said. "But I have a feeling if we don't get this one right, I'll be sleeping on the sofa tonight."

"Sofa, hell," Rachel said. "You'll be lucky to be sleeping in the same hotel."

The moment she spoke the words, Rachel wished she could yank them back. She couldn't believe she'd said that. She couldn't believe it. Everybody laughed again, including Jack. Then he hugged her close and gave her a big, smacking kiss on the cheek, and she wondered how he thought he could do that without her slapping him right across the face. Not only was he making humiliating comments, he was egging her into making them, too, and that made her angrier than anything else.

"Okay, Suzy," Megan said. "This is the bonus question, worth fifteen points. What will Phil say is the color of the panties that you're wearing right now?"

Panties? *Panties?* Rachel felt a sick swoop in her stomach at the mere mention of the word. She couldn't take this. Not one more word of it. She needed to get out of here.

In a daze, she listened as Suzy said "pink." Phil turned up his card to reveal white. Megan turned to Ronnie and Anne. She said "white," and Ronnie's card said "black."

Rachel couldn't believe it. They both missed it. Which meant...

"Okay, Rachel," Megan said. "Looks like you and Jack lucked out. You get this one right, you win. You get it wrong, it's all over for you."

Rachel had a sudden flash of her panties lying on the floor of that linen closet, and embarrassment washed over her again.

No. Get a grip. In spite of the subject matter, it's a straight-forward question, and Jack knows the answer. All he has to do is say it.

"Rachel," Megan said, "for the game, what color panties will Jack say that you're wearing?"

"Blue," she said.

Jack slapped his hand against his forehead, then flipped up his card. Rachel peeked around at it, then looked at him with disbelief.

"Beige?" she said.

"Sorry, sweetheart," he said with a helpless shrug. "It was as close as I could come since the question was faulty."

"Faulty?" Rachel said.

"Yeah," he said, then in a loud stage whisper, "It assumes you're *wearing* panties."

The crowd roared with laughter, catcalls flying left and right. Rachel's stomach churned. Had he actually said that? Had he actually said she wasn't wearing any panties? The laughter reverberated around the room, echoing inside her head, until her cheeks felt as if they were on fire. She'd never been so humiliated in her life. Never.

Megan announced that Phil and Suzy had won the game. She presented them with a bottle of champagne with a big red bow tied around it, and as the crowd clapped for them, she leaned toward Jack and Rachel.

"You guys were a blast," she said. "Thanks for spicing things up."

As Megan walked away, Jack turned to Rachel. "Good job, sweetheart. They loved us. Walter was laughing his head off."

Walter. Oh, God. He'd sat through the whole game, and now he was undoubtedly picturing her lounging on a bed amid salad tongs, a can of whipped cream and half a dozen rolls of duct tape. Wearing no panties. Just the kind of person he wanted to put in charge of the biggest project his firm had ever had.

"I'm a little thirsty," Jack said. "Can I get you something to drink, too?"

She couldn't believe this. He was acting as if nothing had happened here. Nothing at all. How could he be so dense?

Her throat felt so tight she could barely speak. "Yes. Just some ice water for now."

"Coming up."

He gave her a quick kiss, then rose from his chair and headed toward the bar. Rachel got up and headed for the door.

RACHEL SAT ON THE SOFA in their room and stared out the window at the city lights of Silver Springs, tears burning behind her eyes. After the commotion of the game, the room felt eerily quiet, echoing the emptiness she felt in her heart. She'd counted on Jack. She'd counted on him to help her through that game, and instead he'd turned on her, destroying her reputation.

Then suddenly the door to the room flew open and Jack came in.

"Hey, Rachel! Megan said she saw you leave. The party's just getting going. What are you doing up here?"

She refused to look at him. She couldn't. She was angry, hurt, disgraced, and he was the cause of every bit of it.

He strode over to the sofa. "Rachel? What's the matter?"

"I can't believe you did that."

"Did what?"

"Humiliated me like that!"

"What?"

"You heard me. I have to work with those people, and now I'm some kind of laughingstock!"

He looked at her incredulously. "Now, wait a minute. Are you talking about the game we played?"

"What else would I be talking about?"

"Sweetheart, nobody was laughing at you. Not like you think."

"*Everybody* was laughing at me! Those questions...good God! I knew Megan would come up with stuff like that, but did you have to play right into her hands? You couldn't just answer the questions, could you? You had to go right off the deep end, saying all those horrible things!"

"What are you talking about?"

She looked at him with disbelief. "Whipped cream! Salad tongs! Handcuffs! Lord, Jack, you told those people I wasn't wearing any underwear!"

"Come on! Do you think they actually believed those things? They knew they were jokes!"

"No, they didn't!"

"Hey, hold on. Take it easy." He eased over and sat down beside her. "I didn't mean to embarrass you. You told me you overreacted about the panties in the linen closet, so I thought you wouldn't mind—"

"Only you and I knew about that. Tonight you may as well have told everybody."

"You're blowing this *way* out of proportion."

"Do you ever take anything seriously? Do you?"

"Yes! But certainly not something as stupid as this!"

"Of course it's stupid to you. It's not your job we're talking about!"

"In case you didn't notice, that game was set up for laughs. We gave them laughs."

"Laughs. Right. You haven't changed at all, have you? You're still that scared little kid who had to act up to make friends. Maybe it's time you grew up."

The moment the words were out of her mouth, she wished she could take them back. No matter what he'd done to her tonight, she'd had no intention of hurting him, but judging by the hurt expression on his face, that was exactly what she'd done. For a long time neither of them spoke, and the tension between them was excruciating.

"Jack," she said, searching for words, "it's just...it's just that we're so different. I never know what you're going to do. I always have this feeling that every time I turn around, something's going to pop out of your mouth that I'm going to have to deal with. That I won't know *how* to deal with."

"Have you ever stopped to consider that that may be your problem and not mine?"

"Yes, of course I have. I don't have any delusions about what I am, either. I'm way too uptight, way too conservative, and I can't lighten up to save my life. And I know you may not believe this, but I really am envious of how free you are with your life, and how you can talk to people so easily and I can't." She sighed with frustration. "But don't you see? Neither of us is wrong here. We're just not right for each other. You'd drive me nuts inside of a month, and I'd make you crazy, too. I spend my life walking on eggshells, and you're Mr. Spontaneity. In the end it's who we really are, and I think it's best if we face the truth now and not let this go on any longer. We'd make each other miserable."

"Is that what our time together has been? Miserable?"

"No," she admitted. "Of course not. In a lot of ways, it's been wonderful. But—"

"No. Stop right there. No buts. I don't want to hear one more 'but' coming out of your mouth. It's been wonderful. That's all I need to know."

"But, Jack," she said, "what's wonderful for a few days can be excruciating over a lifetime."

Jack blinked with surprise, then turned away, a

wounded expression on his face that made her feel terrible. She knew she'd hurt him, and she'd never, ever wanted to do that, just as he'd never intended to hurt her tonight. Unfortunately that was just further evidence of how deluded she'd been to think that a relationship between them might actually work, when in reality, they were just too different to ever belong together.

He put his elbows on his knees, clasped his hands in front of him, and bowed his head. Rachel hated this because she didn't know what to say. She never knew what to say. Jack was the one who generally had that covered.

Finally he looked up. "You know something, Rachel?"

"What?"

"I think you're probably right."

"I am?"

"Yes. We *would* drive each other crazy, and probably long before a month was out."

She was surprised at his sudden agreement. But then again, why shouldn't he agree? The truth was so plain that anyone could see it.

He sighed regretfully. "Look. Some things are meant to be, and others aren't. I think maybe we just kind of got caught up in the fun of it all, you know? But now that I stop to think about the long haul..." A faint smile came to his lips. "Every day can't be hot sex and curly fries, now can it?"

She turned away. "No, of course not."

"And you know what else? I was wrong for pushing to come on this retreat with you."

"And I was wrong for making up a husband in the first place."

"Yeah, but it showed some genuine creativity," he said with a soft smile. "That I admire." He let out a long breath. "Well, I guess we know where we stand now, don't we?"

"Yes, I guess we do."

Another long silence.

"This is awkward," she said.

"It doesn't have to be. We're in total agreement. What is there to feel awkward about?"

She nodded. And still she felt awkward.

"I guess we'll be heading back to Denver tomorrow morning, huh?" He checked his watch. "It's early yet, but we've had a long day. Did you want to stay up any longer?"

"Uh...no. We might as well go to bed." She nodded toward the bathroom. "I'll go first."

She took her nightgown and robe into the bathroom and closed the door behind her. She stood there a long time, leaning against the door, her clothes clutched to her chest. For some reason, she couldn't stop tears from filling her eyes.

She couldn't believe it. She'd ended it with Jack. Just like that.

She supposed she was lucky they'd played that game. It had told her everything she needed to know about what life with him would be like. He'd made her look ridiculous in front of her boss and co-workers, and in a matter of minutes he'd damaged the professional image that it had taken her years to develop. Nobody would ever be able to look at her again without wondering how many times a week she and her husband had sex, or whether or not she was wearing panties. It was something she was going to have to face from now on.

She got into her nightgown and robe, and when she came out of the bathroom, she was surprised to find Jack on the telephone. He was making a plane reservation. For tomorrow. From Denver to San Antonio.

Already he was moving on.

He put his hand over the phone. "Rachel? When we hit town tomorrow, would you mind giving me a ride to the airport?"

"Uh...sure. Of course."

"There's a flight at two-twenty. Can we make it there by then?"

"Yes. As long as we don't hit any heavy traffic."

He nodded, then told the reservation agent he'd take the flight and gave his credit card information. He hung up the phone, grabbed a pair of pajama bottoms, then disappeared into the bathroom. When he came out bare-chested again, Rachel had a flash of the first night they'd stayed there, when he'd slept on that sofa, and then his voice had drifted across the room...

He collected a blanket and spare pillow from the closet and tossed them onto the sofa.

"You don't have to do that, Jack. I'm sure the sofa's uncomfortable. It's...it's a big bed."

"No, I think this will be best, considering the circumstances."

She nodded. "Maybe you're right."

He lay down on the sofa. She got into bed and turned out the light.

Silence.

She listened for a long time, feeling the most irrational urge to hear his voice in the dark. Then she realized how silly that was. She was longing for that wild, spontaneous side of him that was the very thing she knew she could never stand in a day-to-day relationship. He was being adult about this. She needed to be, too.

She closed her eyes, but sleep didn't come easily. All

she could think about was the man across the room who had taken her someplace she'd never been before and maybe would never go again. In spite of everything, she'd always remember him for that.

15

AT ONE O'CLOCK THE NEXT DAY, Rachel turned her car into Denver International Airport and followed the signs to the departure area of the terminal. All the way back from Silver Springs, she'd been acutely aware of Jack sitting in the passenger seat, making small talk about nothing important, searching for radio stations. In general, he acted as if they were two people who barely knew each other, rather than two people who knew each other as intimately as two people could, and who, for a few moments in time, looked as if they might have a future together.

But the reality was that they didn't. And they never would.

By the time she pulled up to the curb at the terminal, her heart was beating rapid-fire. They got out of the car. A light snow was falling, and the dark clouds that billowed over the mountains told her more was on the way. Jack grabbed his bag from the trunk and slung it over his shoulder.

She stood there shivering in the cold winter wind, feeling as if she should say something—something profound even, about what he'd meant to her. But in the end, the only thing she seemed to be able to do was apologize.

"I'm sorry, Jack," she said. "I'm sorry it couldn't work out."

"Hey, better to find out now than a year from now, right?"

She nodded. Hadn't she essentially told herself that already?

"And we had a good time, right?" He smiled. "Most of the time, anyway?"

"Yeah. We did."

"Have you thought about what you're going to do about our marital status?"

"I'm not sure. I guess I'll wait a few months, then tell everyone that our marriage couldn't withstand the rigors of us being apart all the time, and that we're getting an amicable divorce. If that's okay?"

He nodded. "What does it cost to get an imaginary divorce, anyway? About what it cost for the imaginary Justice of the Peace to marry us?"

She forced a smile. "I suppose that depends on our settlement."

"Well, let me remind you that any alimony you try to stick me for will be equally imaginary, so don't even try it."

What I'm feeling inside right now—is that imaginary, too?

No. She wasn't imagining it. She was going to miss him. More than she ever would have thought.

Then her gaze fell to his warm, sensuous lips—lips that had sent her to heaven with a single kiss—and all at once she had the same outrageous thought that she'd had in that crazy little restaurant in Silver Springs: If she had to go through the rest of her life without ever kissing him again, there was no point in living. Only now, somehow, that thought didn't seem so outrageous after all.

Stop it. It's over. And it's for the best.

He reached into his wallet and pulled out a business card. "Look me up if you're ever in San Antonio again. We can do lunch. And I promise—no more funny drinks with more alcohol than fruit juice, okay?"

She nodded and took the card.

He leaned in and gave her a quick kiss on the cheek. "It's been real fun, sweetheart. Maybe we can do it again in another six months."

Then he turned and headed toward the terminal without so much as a backward glance.

Rachel stared after him, watching as he went through the sliding doors into the building. She stuck his business card into the side pocket of her purse, then turned and got back into her car. She sat there a moment, feeling as if she was going to cry.

How could he do this to her? How could he be so nonchalant about the time they'd spent together? It wasn't something she wanted for a lifetime, but it had been special to her. How could he act as if it had been no big deal?

Because that was Jack. Never serious about anything for very long. And he was right. Better to find out now than a year from now that it wasn't going to work, before she was so emotionally tied to him that letting go would be a miserable experience.

As if it wasn't miserable enough already.

She started her car. She happened to glance back, and to her surprise, she saw Jack staring out the window of the terminal. Just standing there, staring at her. Then he turned and walked away.

She watched the window for a moment more, then put her car in gear. She drove back to Denver, and for the rest of the day, she sat around her condo in a daze, feeling an empty spot inside her that she had no idea how to fill. And when she went to bed that night, in that twilight state between waking and sleep, she found herself listening once again for a voice in the dark.

A voice that would never be there again.

ON MONDAY, RACHEL ARRIVED at work before anyone else, then sequestered herself in her office all morning, hoping to avoid as many people as she could for as long as she could. She just wasn't up to the looks she was sure to get from her fellow employees—looks that said they wondered if she carried duct tape around in her purse for any unexpected bondage emergencies.

At least a dozen times before noon, she turned around to look at Jack's picture on her credenza. Then finally she had enough of her own inability to concentrate, and she grabbed it and stuffed it into her bottom desk drawer. Logic told her that Jack Kellerman was the worst thing that could possibly have happened to her.

That damned logic thing again. *Logic.* She'd truly come to hate the very word, because if he was really so wrong for her, then why did she miss him so much?

Around lunchtime, her phone rang. It was Megan, calling her from the front desk.

"Hey, Rachel," she said. "Walter just got into the office, and he wants to see you."

Rachel felt a shot of apprehension. "He does? What about?"

"No idea, but he wants to see you right now."

"Tell him I'll be there in a minute."

Rachel hung up the phone, and already her palms were sweating. Walter didn't summon people—he was more of a "drop by your office" kind of guy. This had to have something to do with the retreat. Or with the project manager position. Or both. And she couldn't imagine that the news was going to be good.

She rose from her chair and headed for Walter's office, where she found him digging through a file cabinet. He extracted a file, then shut the drawer.

"Walter? You wanted to see me?"

He turned around. "Rachel! Yes. Come in."

As she stepped into his office, he checked his watch. "Sorry for dragging you down to my office, but I'm already late for a lunch meeting, and I had to dig up this file. But since I stopped by, I thought I'd go ahead and give you the news."

"News?"

"I've made my decision. The project manager position for the new hotel and casino in Reno is yours."

Rachel nearly fainted. "What?"

Walter grabbed his briefcase from his guest chair and put it on his desk. "With your technical expertise, I was looking for a reason to give you that job. I can't tell you how pleased I was when you gave one to me."

"I—I don't understand."

"I have to tell you, Rachel, that when I hired you six months ago, it was a tough decision, because...well, truthfully, I found you a bit cold. But your résumé was so impeccable that I took a chance. Now I'm glad I did." He unzipped a pocket of his briefcase and stuffed the file inside. "You see, I have a radically different view on corporate life than the average manager. I believe that the employees who play together stay together. And that goes for couples, too. Seeing you and Jack together on the retreat, particularly when you played that silly game on the last night, made me realize that you have that kind of attitude in your marriage. I don't think you'll have any trouble translating that to your new job, as well."

Rachel couldn't believe this. Walter had changed his opinion about her because of Jack?

"Uh...thank you, Walter. I appreciate your confidence in me."

"I saw another side of you at that retreat," Walter said, zipping his briefcase. "You're much more engaging than I ever realized." He smiled. "I really enjoyed our conversation on Thursday night."

Thursday night. Jack again. She remembered how he'd steered the conversation around to get her and Walter talking about the Civil War, then taken Phil out of the mix so he wouldn't get in the way. And all of it had made her feel wonderful.

"I must admit," Rachel said, "that I thought Phil Wardman would be your first choice."

Walter raised an eyebrow. "Just between you and me, the more I was around Phil socially, the more I realized that he can be a bit...well, overbearing. By the time the retreat was over, his behavior, as well as yours, had made my decision very clear."

Rachel nodded solemnly, even as her stomach was fluttering with excitement.

Walter checked his watch again. "I've got to run. We'll talk more about it later. I just wanted to give you the news and to tell you congratulations. We'll be starting on the project next month."

"I'll be looking forward to it."

Rachel walked as far as the reception desk with Walter. He headed for the door, then turned back. "Be sure to send my regards to Jack. It was great to finally get to meet him. I hope we'll be seeing more of him?"

"Uh...yes. Of course."

"He's a good man. Hang on to him."

She gave him a shaky smile. "I will."

Walter left the office and stepped into the elevator lobby. As the glass door closed behind him, Megan leaned over the reception desk.

"So what did he want?" Megan asked.

Rachel turned around slowly, still stunned. "I got the project manager job."

"You did? That's great! Phil is going to hate you. Have you told Jack yet?"

Rachel felt numb. "I won't be telling Jack."

"Huh?"

"Jack's not here."

"Where is he?"

"San Antonio."

"And...?"

"And...nothing."

"What do you mean, nothing?"

"He's there, I'm here. That's it."

Megan's eyes grew wide as searchlights. "Oh, no. Don't tell me you broke up."

Hearing those words come out of Megan's mouth made them seem that much more real, and that much more painful.

"Yeah," she said weakly. "We broke up."

"You mean to tell me that you let that man get *away?*"

"We had a fight."

"A fight? About what?"

"Something...something...oh, God, Megan. Something that I'm not sure matters anymore." Tears sprang to Rachel's eyes, and suddenly she felt light-headed, as if she couldn't catch a solid breath. "I'm not sure it ever mattered."

"What are you talking about?"

She was talking about her misguided idea that Jack was bad for her. That all his teasing and laughter and attempts to bring out those qualities in her would somehow eventually ruin her life. But it hadn't ruined her life at all. Getting that job, and knowing the reason why, blasted away all her hang-ups and misconceptions, until finally she saw the truth.

Jack had been right. About everything. During that

game, those people hadn't been laughing at her. Nobody had taken it seriously.

Nobody but her.

How blind could she possibly have been?

All at once, she knew another truth. She knew with total clarity what was important to her, and it wasn't a high-profile promotion, a prestigious career, or an uptight professional reputation. What was most important to her was a handsome, sexy, sometimes outrageous but always kind and gentle man who made her feel more alive than she ever had in her life, who brought out the best in her for all the world to see. What kind of fool was she to give him up?

But what if she'd driven him away for good by all the terrible things she'd said? What if he truly never wanted to see her again?

He'd made such light of the fact that they'd ever had a relationship in the first place. He'd made it quite clear when she dropped him off at the airport that he'd already written her off. How could he have done that? After everything that had been between them, how could he just...

Then suddenly she remembered something they'd talked about in the lounge of that hotel in Silver Springs. Something deep, something heartfelt, and all at once the truth of the situation hit her so hard that her knees went weak and she had to stumble to the sofa in the reception area to sit down.

Why hadn't she seen it before?

I know I make a joke out of everything because, you know, if you keep it light, keep them laughing, then when it comes time to say goodbye...

Then all at once, she remembered glancing back and seeing Jack staring out the window of the terminal at Denver International. He wasn't smiling. He wasn't laughing.

He was saying goodbye. And it was breaking his heart.

For several seconds, Rachel just sat there, her palms sweating, her head spinning. How could she have thought he didn't care?

A breathless, almost painful sensation overtook her. She put her hand to her throat, feeling her own heart breaking as surely as his had. She had to tell him. She had to tell him how wrong she'd been about him, about them, about everything. She only prayed she wouldn't be too late.

She got up from the sofa, rushed to her office and grabbed her purse, relieved when she found Jack's business card still in the side pocket.

Megan appeared at her office doorway. "Rachel! What are you doing?"

She spun around. "Megan! Will you make me a plane reservation?"

"A plane reservation? Where to?"

"San Antonio."

Megan's eyes lit up. "Oh, yeah? How soon do you want to leave?"

"If you can find me a flight leaving yesterday, I'd appreciate it."

Megan grinned. "You got it."

JACK GOT TO THE WORK SITE at the Wimberly Building by eight o'clock sharp, even though it had taken every bit of energy he had to drag himself out of bed. If he hadn't already missed a few days on the job, he might have just stayed home, but he felt he owed it to Tom since he'd disappeared so suddenly last week. But now that it was approaching noon and he'd accomplished next to nothing, he wasn't sure why he'd bothered.

He put his finger to the switch of his power saw and cut

through a two-by-four. He lay the saw down, then hoisted the board to his shoulder and swung around.

"Hey! Look out!"

Startled by the voice behind him, Jack turned again. Tom ducked, apparently for the second time, to avoid being knocked in the head.

"Will you give me that?" Tom said, yanking the board right out of Jack's hands. "What's the matter with you? First thing this morning, you saw halfway through a sawhorse. Then you leave a tape measure lying on a staircase for somebody to find with their foot. Now you're trying to take me out with a two-by-four. I swear you're going to kill somebody before the day's out. You want to tell me what's the matter?"

"Nothing's the matter."

"Nothing. Right." Tom tossed the two-by-four to the ground. "You do realize that this board you just cut is about two feet too short, don't you?"

Jack stared down at it. "Sorry. I'll cut another one."

"Will you just stop? We can't afford to lose half a dozen more." Tom took a step toward Jack and gave him a nononsense look. "Don't you think it's about time you told me what happened in Colorado?"

Jack looked away. "Things didn't work out. That's all."

"Well, then, there's no problem, is there? Easy come, easy go."

Jack slowly turned his gaze back to meet Tom's, his jaw tight, his expression somber.

"Okay," Tom said. "So I guess there must have been a little more to it than that."

A lot more. A lot more than Jack had ever counted on. The time he'd spent with Rachel at that resort had turned out to be even more incredible than he ever could have imagined. And now she wanted to have nothing to do with him.

But he had to face the truth. It was his own damned fault that she felt that way.

You're still that sad little boy who has to cut up to make friends. Maybe it's time you grew up.

That had hurt like hell, because there was a heaping dose of truth in it. *Trust me.* He'd said those words at least a dozen times over the four days they were at that ski resort. And she had. Then he'd betrayed her confidence. He told her he'd help her during that game, and what did he do? He played it for laughs because that's what made *him* comfortable. He'd left her right out in the cold in a situation that he knew was one of the hardest things in the world for her to cope with. Left her to feel as if she was the brunt of a great big joke.

He knew that wasn't really true. Everyone had enjoyed the game, and they'd been a real hit with the crowd. He knew that, and so did everyone else there.

Everyone but Rachel.

He'd wanted desperately to keep talking that night, to tell her just how wrong she was and that they really did belong together. But then she'd cut him right to the quick.

What's wonderful for a few days can be excruciating over a lifetime.

Excruciating. That was how she saw him. Even now, just thinking about the words she'd spoken nearly ripped his heart out. But he hadn't been able to tell her that. All he'd been able to do is agree with her that their relationship had no chance, when he knew that nothing was further from the truth. But the second he felt that goodbye coming, he knew he had to keep his distance any way he could.

The way he always did.

But now the very thought that he'd joked his way right through their last moments together made him sick to his stomach. What he'd been desperate to do instead was tell her straight from his heart how he really felt. And he just hadn't had the guts to do it.

"Actually, Tom, I may have made the biggest mistake of my life. Only now I don't know how to fix it. I don't even know if it can be fixed."

"Aw, come on! You, Mr. Charming, can't get back in a woman's good graces? That'd be a first."

"Believe me—my charming side is the last thing she wants to see right about now."

"Why don't you call her?" Tom suggested.

He could do that. He could talk to her. He could tell her all day long how sorry he was for what he'd done and how good they would be together, but when it came right down to it, his actions had spoken louder than words. He'd shown her that what she'd feared all along was true—that somehow, if he hung around long enough, he'd make a mess of her life. Sadly, that was exactly what he'd done.

"Calling her won't do any good," he told Tom.

"Well, you'd better do something, and fast, or we're going to have to take out extra liability insurance."

But what could he do? He'd told Tom the truth. Calling her wasn't going to get him anywhere. He had to do more than that.

That was the answer.

Jack froze for a moment, playing a possible solution over in his mind, and it didn't take long for him to realize that it was the only shot he had.

If actions spoke louder than words, then it was time for him to take action.

16

AT FOUR O'CLOCK THAT afternoon, Rachel raced into the terminal at Denver International, a shopping bag draped over her arm, dragging her carry-on behind her. Traffic had been heavy, and at the rate she was going, she was going to be late for her flight, which meant that it would be another day before she could get to San Antonio, another day before she could apologize, another day before she could make everything right that she'd made so wrong.

Fortunately the crowd at the airport was light, and check-in took only a few minutes. After leaving the counter, she followed the signs toward her gate, stepping onto an escalator that would take her in the direction.

As the escalator descended, she took a deep breath, then checked her watch. It was a little after four. Her flight didn't leave for another half hour, but if she didn't get to the gate in the next few minutes and check in there, they could take her seat away from her.

Then, for no reason at all, she glanced toward the escalator beside her, and what she saw made her heart leap.

Jack?

As she was going down, he was going up.

She was so stunned that she just stared at him, thinking it couldn't be him, that she had to be seeing things, that he couldn't possibly be in this airport right now. But then he turned and saw her, and his eyes flew open wide with surprise.

"Rachel!"

As she continued to descend, he immediately spun around and started down the up escalator. Like a fish swimming against the tide, he excused himself around the people in his way, and when the overnight bag slung over his shoulder became a liability, he ditched it, leaving it to continue up the escalator while he worked his way down. Rachel was so astonished to see him and so preoccupied with watching him that she nearly tripped and fell when the escalator she was on spilled her out at the bottom. She'd just righted herself and her luggage when Jack made a final leap off the other escalator and rushed over to her. He came to a quick halt, breathing hard, then glanced down at her carry-on luggage.

"Damn it!" he muttered.

"What?"

"You're probably going on a business trip, or something, aren't you?" He paced away a couple of strides, gritting his teeth, then paced back. "I should have called first. I *knew* I should have called first!"

"Jack?" she said, her heart beating wildly. "What are you doing here?"

"Listen to me, Rachel. I made a big mistake the last night of the retreat. I let you tell me it was over between us. Well, it's not over. At least, it's not over until I say everything I have to say."

"Jack—"

"You asked me if I ever take anything seriously. The answer to that is *hell, yes.* I take what's between us very seriously. I've never been more serious about anything in my life."

"Jack—"

"No. Don't talk. I flew a thousand miles to say this, and you're not going to interrupt."

Rachel closed her mouth.

"About the game we played that last night of the re-treat...you were right. I knew how you felt about being up there in front of all those people, and I should have helped you through it. I didn't. I went for the laugh and totally disregarded how you felt about it. And if I screwed up your reputation in front of your boss and co-workers, I'm sorry about that, too. You don't know how much. But there was a time when being in social situations was as hard for me as it is for you, and cutting up like an obnoxious kid has always been my stupid way of coping with it. But I'm sure as hell willing to grow out of all that if you'll give me a chance."

"Jack—"

"I'm not through yet." He moved closer still, dropping his voice. "The time we spent together in San Antonio really threw me. I'd fought my whole life not to get too close to anyone, and then all the sudden, there you were, and I was feeling things I'd never felt before. I mean, why do you think I practically killed myself in downtown Denver traffic to catch up to you so I wouldn't lose you again? Why do you think I fought so hard to go on that retreat with you? It was because I was afraid that if I didn't get to spend some time with you, you'd disappear from my life again, and couldn't stand the thought of that. I want to be with you, Rachel. From now on. I have no idea how we can work things out so we can be together, but I want to give it a try."

Then he took her by the shoulders and stared at her. "I don't know if you've figured it out yet or not because I've danced around it about fifty different ways here, but I'm in love with you. I think I've even been in love with you since that first night in San Antonio. And no matter what happens from here on out, I'm still going to love you. Nothing is ever going to change that."

Finally he was silent. Rachel swallowed hard. Had he just said he loved her?

Yes. He had. He'd just laid his heart right out in front of her, and not a joke on earth could cover it up. For once, not a shadow of humor sparked in his eyes, not a single witty comment came out of his mouth. He was totally, thoroughly, deadly serious.

"Are you finished?" she asked.

He slid his hands away from her shoulders. "I don't know," he said. "Am I?"

She handed him her airline ticket.

"What's this?" he asked.

"Look at it."

He opened it up. He glanced at the face of the ticket, then looked back at her with surprise. "You're going to San Antonio?"

"Well, I guess I'm not now. You saved me the trip."

"You were coming to see me?"

"You told me to look you up sometime, didn't you?" She shrugged. "I thought we'd do lunch."

"Do lunch?"

He just stood there, staring at her, never even cracking a smile because he was so preoccupied with something so much more important to him that it went right over his head. And she loved him for it.

"I have a lot to say to you, too, Jack. First of all, I got the project manager job."

"You did? That's great!"

"Because of you."

"Me?"

"Walter told me he wasn't too sure about even hiring

me in the first place to work there, much less giving me the new job, because he was afraid I wouldn't relate well to other people. But then he saw me on that retreat. With you. Connecting to people. Interacting with people. Even making people laugh." She paused. "You were right. It was what Walter wanted. And you know what? It's what I want, too. I was just too blind to see it."

Jack smiled. "I'm glad you got the job."

"I'm quitting Davidson Design."

"You're *what?*"

"You were right about that, too. My heart isn't in it. And I'm not going to live the rest of my life feeling no passion for the work I do."

"Rachel, wait a minute. I never wanted to come between you and your career."

"You're not. Like you said, there are probably a hundred other firms I could work for who would think twice before they disfigure the American landscape." She smiled. "Some of them might even be in San Antonio."

Jack couldn't believe it. She was talking about coming to San Antonio? Permanently?

"Actually," she said, "I was on my way there right now to beg you to forgive me for every stupid thing I said and did the last night of that retreat. For all those terrible things I said to you." She took his hands in hers. "Life with you wouldn't be excruciating, Jack. It would be *amazing.*"

He didn't dare get his hopes up that she actually meant everything she was saying, that she intended to quit her job, that she planned to move to San Antonio, and that she wanted a life with him. He was a born optimist, but even he wasn't naive enough to believe that many good things could come in one package.

"Are you sure about all this, sweetheart?"

"Yes, Jack. All of it. Do you want me to prove it?"

"Prove it?"

"Yeah. Hold on just a minute."

She turned her back to him and dug around in a shopping bag that was draped over her arm. When she turned back around, to his utter astonishment, she was wearing a Groucho Marx mask—the glasses, big nose, the mustache, the bushy eyebrows. All of it.

"So what do you think?" she asked, holding her arms out. "Funny, huh?"

For a moment, all Jack could do was stare in amazement. The sight of Rachel perpetrating one of the most ridiculous gags of all time was just about more than his brain could comprehend. But then he saw her blue eyes peering at him through those big, ugly glasses, and he realized that no matter what mask she put on, he'd always know the real woman behind it.

"Actually," he told her, smiling contentedly, "I don't think I've ever seen you look more beautiful."

She slapped her arms back down against her sides, slumping with frustration. "I go for a laugh, you give me a compliment?" She sighed dramatically. "Oh, boy. I really *am* lousy at this kind of thing."

"Now, don't you worry," he said. "It took me a lot of years to get like this. These things take time."

She smiled softly. "I love you, Jack."

Then she eased up next to him, and with everyone in the vicinity looking on, she wrapped her arms around his neck and kissed him.

And kissed him.

And *kissed* him.

It was a great big, full-blown, public display of affection that had to be making jaws drop all over the place, and Jack decided that if she was kissing him in the middle of

Denver International Airport wearing a Groucho mask, maybe his optimism wasn't unwarranted after all.

Finally she pulled away, and he slid the glasses off her face. "Okay, sweetheart. Enough with the glasses. You're starting to embarrass me."

"Did the kiss embarrass you, too?" she asked.

"Yes." He paused. "Would you please embarrass me some more?"

She slipped her arms around his neck and brushed her lips against his. "Are people watching?" she whispered.

"Uh-huh. About half the population of Denver."

She kissed him again, and Jack knew there was no way he was ever letting this woman get away from him again.

"Do you think it's possible," he said, "that sometime in the near future, you might consider turning your imaginary husband into the real thing?"

She stared at him, dumbfounded. "Are you asking me to marry you?"

"Yes. That's exactly what I'm doing."

A smile slowly spread across her face. "You'll have to buy me a real diamond, you know. I don't want people thinking you're cheap."

"I suppose you're also going to expect flowers on every birthday with a mushy card from your loving husband."

"Absolutely. But you'll be pleased to know that the job does come with a few perks."

"Oh, yeah? What kind of perks?"

"You'll see."

They left the airport hand in hand, and before the day was out, she'd shown him every one of them.

**Receive 2 FREE Trade books with 4 proofs
of purchase from Harlequin Temptation® books.**

HARLEQUIN®
Temptation.

You will receive:

Dangerous Desires: Three complete novels by
Jayne Ann Krentz, Barbara Delinsky and Anne Stuart

and

Legacies of Love: Three complete novels by
Jayne Ann Krentz, Stella Cameron and Heather Graham

**Simply complete the order form and mail to:
"Temptation 2 Free Trades Offer"**

In U.S.A.	In CANADA
P.O. Box 9057	P.O. Box 622
3010 Walden Avenue	Fort Erie, Ontario
Buffalo, NY 14269-9057	L2A 5X3

YES! Please send me *Dangerous Desires* and *Legacies of Love,* without
cost or obligation except shipping and handling. Enclosed are 4 proofs
of purchase from September or October 2002 Harlequin Temptation
books and $3.75 shipping and handling fees. New York State residents
must add applicable sales tax to shipping and handling charge.
Canadian residents must add 7% GST to shipping and handling charge.

Name (PLEASE PRINT)

Address   Apt. #

City   State/Prov.   Zip/Postal Code

TEMPTATION 2 FREE TRADES OFFER TERMS
To receive your FREE trade books, please complete the above
form. Mail it to us with 4 proofs of purchase, one of which can
be found in the lower right-hand corner of this page. Requests
must be received no later than November 30, 2002. Please
include $3.75 for shipping and handling fees and applicable
taxes as stated above. The 2 FREE Trade books are valued at
$12.95 U.S./$14.95 CAN. each. All orders are subject to
approval. Terms and prices are subject to change without
notice. Please allow 6-8 weeks for delivery. Offer good in
Canada and the U.S. only. Offer good while quantities last.
Offer limited to one per household.

Temptation.
2 FREE TRADES OFFER
One Proof of Purchase

HARLEQUIN®
Makes any time special ®

HTPOPFT

Princes...Princesses...
London Castles...New York Mansions...
To live the life of a royal!

In 2002, Harlequin Books lets you escape to a
world of royalty with these royally themed titles:

Temptation:
January 2002—*A Prince of a Guy* (#861)
February 2002—*A Noble Pursuit* (#865)

American Romance:
The Carradignes: American Royalty (Editorially linked series)
March 2002—*The Improperly Pregnant Princess* (#913)
April 2002—*The Unlawfully Wedded Princess* (#917)
May 2002—*The Simply Scandalous Princess* (#921)
November 2002—*The Inconveniently Engaged Prince* (#945)

Intrigue:
The Carradignes: A Royal Mystery (Editorially linked series)
June 2002—*The Duke's Covert Mission* (#666)

Chicago Confidential
September 2002—*Prince Under Cover* (#678)

The Crown Affair
October 2002—*Royal Target* (#682)
November 2002—*Royal Ransom* (#686)
December 2002—*Royal Pursuit* (#690)

Harlequin Romance:
June 2002—*His Majesty's Marriage* (#3703)
July 2002—*The Prince's Proposal* (#3709)

Harlequin Presents:
August 2002—*Society Weddings* (#2268)
September 2002—*The Prince's Pleasure* (#2274)

Duets:
September 2002—*Once Upon a Tiara/Henry Ever After* (#83)
October 2002—*Natalia's Story/Andrea's Story* (#85)

Celebrate a year of royalty with
Harlequin Books!

Available at your favorite retail outlet.

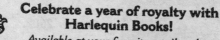

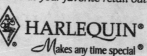

HARLEQUIN®
Makes any time special ®

Visit us at www.eHarlequin.com

HSROY02